WET DOGS DON'T RIDE

—DAVID A. ESTES—

Cover Design: Sharon Kizziah-Holmes

Paperback-Press
an imprint of A & S Publishing
A & S Holmes, Inc.

.

ISBN-10: 1-945669-08-X
ISBN-13: 978-1-945669-08-8

CHAPTER 1

The Little Big Horn

Dan Redford felt the weight of a dead body drop on top of him. A Lakota rifle slug had struck his left shoulder and he could hardly move.

The lifeless, contorted face he recognized as Lieutenant Colonel George Armstrong Custer.

With a scornful shake of his head, Redford rolled the body aside.

Custer had perceived himself as an invincible hero. He died trying to prove it, and took with him a regiment of good men to wherever the gods deliver the souls of dead warriors.

Tuesday June 26, 1876, arrived as quietly as a cat on cotton. The silence of dawn was broken only by the lonesome call of a mourning dove.

Like a duck hunter scanning a foggy river, the

rising sun peeked over the edge of the world, surveying the Little Big Horn River, as if it knew what took place there. Like it came to comfort with its soothing glow the two-hundred-sixty-nine U. S. Cavalrymen sprawled on the eastern slope of the river. Like it knew two-hundred-sixty-eight of them were dead.

Time and circumstances dimmed the memory of the legend of army scout Dan Redford, the only man who greeted the sweltering Montana morning with breath in his body. For two days and two nights, Redford survived what he thought hell must be like, dodging the flying arrows and screaming bullets of the amassed Teton tribes.

He pondered whether giving up his deputy's badge to scout for the army was the smart thing to do. He did it because the army paid more than the badge. Forty bucks a month were not to be sneezed at. Twice as much as he made as Demp Whitton's deputy.

Redford checked the bloody gash in his shoulder. The bullet missed the bone, leaving a hole in the flesh from front to back. The pain was not unbearable, but the shoulder was a bloody mass.

He slid his right hand from the shoulder to the wrist. The shirt sleeve was matted with sticky, drying blood. He grabbed a handful of dry grass and wiped the blood from his hand.

When the bullet struck, he flattened out on his stomach and stayed there motionless, hardly breathing, until the tribes moved out in the eerie soundlessness between night and day.

They did what they came to do–protecting from

the white man the land they roamed freely for countless generations, the land the Treaties said belonged to them. But the government proved that treaties, like promises, were sometimes broken, and waged a campaign to drive the Indians from the territory they called their own since the first sunrise.

The battle was finally over. With no more white warriors to kill, the Indians gathered up the bodies of their dead braves and moved out before dawn silent as the death they left behind.

Peering beyond the body of the dead colonel, Redford looked around for signs of life. There were none–only cavalrymen, strewn over the eastern slope sweeping down to the river's edge. Wide-eyed, twisted faces of dead comrades reflected shock. They died on a dry, blood-saturated hillside by a river they never heard of, in a place they never heard of that somebody told them was Montana.

Along the far side of the Little Big Horn, a whirling breeze scattered what was left of the Indian staging area, now deserted, no longer threatening.

Custer's ambition was to destroy the village without losing a man. He didn't live long enough to find out the combined tribes' tenacious, centuries-old heritage, fighting spirit, and determination to defend what was theirs, proved how wrong he was.

Before the first shot was fired, Redford had warned Custer of the four thousand Indians ranged along the banks of the Little Big Horn River. He tried to persuade him he couldn't defeat the tribes with a handful of cavalry. "Attacking them would be as foolhardy as a mouse taking on a raccoon,"

Redford said. But the colonel's mind was made up, his ears closed to any voice but his own.

Viewing the body of the dead Seventh Cavalry commander, Redford gave his head a derisive shake. "Brash bastard," he said to nobody and nothing, except for the early morning breeze fluttering the yellow hair of the fallen colonel. "He thought he could conquer the world," Redford reflected bitterly.

But he conquered nothing, and left two-hundred-sixty-eight U. S. Cavalry dead on a barren hillside. At West Point, Custer had finished last in a class of thirty-four. He learned how to be an officer and a gentleman, how to read a map, and how to survive in the desert. What he didn't learn was how to apply common sense to a given situation–like not going into battle, challenging the mettle of four thousand irate Indians with the odds of one-hundred-fifty to one.

Custer led his regiment into the Indians' homeland with little thought he might sacrifice the lives of his men for a futile cause. The Sioux and Cheyenne waged a fierce campaign to fight for what was theirs with courage and fire power that Custer miscalculated.

In what was to be the last great battle between the Indian and the white man, the tribes were brought together by Sitting Bull's call for them to desert the reservations and join forces at the Little Big Horn River.

Camped along the banks of the river, they waited and watched, calculating how many white soldiers they'd have to kill to keep the territory the Treaties promised for "as long as the wind shall blow, and the grass shall grow."

Obsessed with an unscratchable itch to destroy the tribes he regarded as savages, Custer shortened their wait. His service as a cavalry officer during the Civil War, and as leader of the Washita massacre of the Southern Cheyenne in Indian Territory, he considered insufficient to serve his purpose.

Critics scoffed at the thirty-seven-year-old Ohioan's ambition to be elected president of the United States. Custer harbored the notion of storming the Little Big Horn, demolishing the Indians with a contingent of U.S. Cavalry. If he succeeded, his political stock would soar, he believed, and would throw wide open the doors of the White House for his triumphant entry.

Crow and Cree scouts knew the Teton tribes had come together to fight for their land.

Redford urged Custer to trust the scouts' report.

The arrogant colonel trusted no counsel but his own, determined to carry out the attack on what proved to be strategically naive and suicidal. Custer considered himself superior to the Indians, regarding them as less than human. The Indians, he convinced himself, were soulless savages devoid of the spirit to fight. Victory would be swift and complete.

Redford knew better. He didn't agree with the government's plot to force the Indians off their land, but the Army paid him to scout, and that's what he did.

Even so, when the treaties were violated, and gold miners invaded the Black Hills which the

Indians had been assured the right to roam freely until time ran out, Redford sympathized with the plight of the natives.

Sitting Bull, adviser to the tribes, had listened to the words Redford brought from the white man's commanders. Dispatched to advise the chief of the white warriors' coming, Redford outlined a plan by which the great Sioux chief could persuade the renegade braves, who frequently attacked U.S. Army units, to return to the reservations.

Spreading his arms wide, hands high in a gesture of peace, Redford had ridden alone into the Indian camp. Though recognized by some of the braves as a white warrior, they dared not challenge him. Redford's mission was to parley with the chief.

"You do not know our people," Sitting Bull said, seated cross-legged beside the campfire. "You do not know our ways, yet you drive us from our hunting grounds. You war against us, kill our braves, and drive away our women and children."

"I don't agree with what they want to do," Redford had said, "but the white warrior will come again, this time with many men, horses and guns."

"Then we will fight!" Sitting Bull protested in a strong voice. Stabbing the air with a folded fist, he emphasized his conviction. "Our gods will protect us!"

And so they had.

CHAPTER 2

Who're you going to kill?

Emitt Coldwater was a slender young man with a week's growth of beard and a shock of black hair. He didn't know how long it took him to ride from San Saba, Texas, to Whiskey Flats, Kansas, but he was glad the ride was over.

Landing in someone else's town, instinct told him to take a look along the street splitting the town east and west. The rigs and mounts tethered along both sides of Parker Street were no different from other cow towns dotting the west.

With a satisfied nod, he dropped a rein over the hitch rack, and strolled into the Bang Tail Saloon. The first thing he laid eyes on was a red headed woman behind the bar. Her name was Eden Fletcher. Her smoky grey eyes flecked with gold caused many a cowboy to forget how tough he was.

Wiping whiskey drippings off the mahogany bar she ordered from Kansas City the day after she buried her husband, Eden looked up to see the young man swaggering her way.

Before she got to be the boss lady at the Bang Tail Saloon in Whiskey Flats, Eden was a strip dancer in a Kansas City casino. One night a man named Matt Fletcher waited for her at the stage door. He introduced himself, and coaxed Eden into joining him for supper at his hotel. During the evening he convinced her she was too good to be dancing naked in a cheap gambling hall.

Fletcher offered her a job as the featured entertainer at his Bang Tail Saloon. He promised she would never have to strip again, only sing and dance, for which he would pay her well. Ending a career of exposing her bare skin to satisfy the lascivious leers of whiskey-sodden patrons, for Eden was a hovering dream, with little hope it would ever come true. Whatever else happened, escaping Jack Claxton would be worth the risk. Fletcher's proposal sounded good, and she said yes.

At sunrise, Fletcher handed Eden up into his fancy surrey with the fringe on top. He hauled her to the wide open spaces of western Kansas and installed her as the star entertainer at his Bang Tail Saloon.

Three times each night Eden sang and danced, twisting and turning her shapely curves, eliciting the applause of saucer-eyed cowpokes who never before witnessed such a performance. At no time was she required to bare her body.

Not many moons came and went before folks were aware that Fletcher viewed his star entertainer as more than an attractive lady gracing the stage of his saloon. It was old news, therefore, when Fletcher finally worked up the gumption to ask Eden to marry him. Once again she said "yes"–the same word she uttered the first time he and Eden met. Most surprised of all was Matt Fletcher when she agreed to marry him.

To Eden, "yes" meant this might be her chance to put down the roots she longed for, enjoying the benefits of a normal life.

After the wedding, Eden stripped only in her husband's bedroom. Twice her age, after seven wet weeks, Fletcher died trying to satisfy her bedtime appetite. Doc Bowman pronounced Matt dead of physical exhaustion–and disappointment that he failed in his quest to prove himself capable of fulfilling his new wife's physical needs.

George Haskell, the local Baptist preacher, presided at the graveside, threw the last shovel of dirt on top of the casket, and Eden suddenly became the sole proprietor of the Bang Tail Saloon. Retiring as singer and dancer, Eden assumed the position of owner and head bartender of the town's most popular saloon.

Sight of her pouty mouth and enticing bosom set Coldwater's innards to squirming.

"Howdy, stranger," Eden greeted him with a disarming smile. "Tell me what I can do for you. If I can't do it, I'll find somebody who can."

She set a glass and a bottle on the bar in front of this man she didn't know, who wandered in from where she also didn't know, but she had no trouble detecting the irritation of a raw throat that rode in with him.

Coldwater's eyes were locked on the provocative mounds of Eden's bosom.

"How far," he said, "would a man have to go to find a whorehouse around here?"

"I wouldn't know," was Eden's casual reply. She didn't have to be told that an urge to dampen his dry throat was not the only thing he brought with him into her saloon. "I never felt the need for one," she said.

"How about a church?" said Coldwater, conceding the round.

"We've got one of those," Eden said. "It's down the street to your right on your way out. Keep walking far enough west and you'll run in the front door."

"Who's the preacher?" Coldwater said.

"George Haskell. Go talk to George. He'll tell you about whorehouses."

Coldwater poured himself a glassful from the bottle and threw it back. "You know a man named Redford? I know a man named Dan Redford. Is that the one you mean?"

"That's the one."

"Why do you want to know?" Eden said.

"I've got a little business to take care of with him."

"What kind of business?"

"I'm gonna kill him."

"You're going to kill Redford?" she asked, her face coated with wide-eyed disbelief.

"That's right."

"Do you know Dan Redford?" she asked.

"No, we never met."

"But you're going to kill him. Or are you just thinking about it?"

"I aim to get it done."

"Does he know that?" she asked.

"Not yet."

"You're pretty sure of yourself, aren't you?"

He downed another drink, and answered with a wry smile. "Is he a friend of yours?"

"You asked me if I knew him, and I said yes."

She grabbed the bottle and took it away. She'd had enough of the brash young stranger, and didn't want him downing any more of her high priced booze that he hadn't paid for. "I'll tell you what, if the business you've got in mind is as serious as you make it sound, you better hustle up all the luck and backbone you can find if you go up against Redford. He won't die easy."

"We'll see." Coldwater tossed some coins on the bar.

"He's pretty good with a gun," Eden said.

"So am I." Coldwater patted the revolver laced to his right thigh. "I'm faster than him."

"Fast won't count for much if you're dead," she said. "He'll kill you before you clear leather."

He dropped a corner of his mouth in a one-sided grin, bottomed up his glass, and headed for the door.

"What's your name?" Eden said.

Coldwater answered with a casual wave.

Eden watched him go. "Good looking boots,"

she called after him.

Coldwater did an abrupt about face.

"You tangle with Redford," Eden said, "and they won't look so good."

He paused, stared at her a moment. He had more to say, but turned away without saying it.

With a dubious shake of her head, Eden wondered if she would see him again. "Not likely alive," she said, answering her own question, "if he goes up against Redford."

CHAPTER 3

Welcome, stranger

Oscar Doke looked out between the dirty smudges on the front window of his hardware store. He squinted his sixty-year-old eyes for a closer look at what they were trying to get him to believe–a black man riding a white horse down the middle of Parker Street.

Parker Street split the town east to west, named as a memorial to Judson Parker, the first man ever shot and killed in Whiskey Flats. Glaring at Parker from the other side of the poker table, an irate wrangler had accused him of card-sharking, and shot him dead in his chair. Parker had no chance to plead his case.

Oscar Doke, sipping at a glass of lemonade at a nearby table, viewed the Parker shooting with shocked disbelief. Now, here was this black man riding a white horse down the middle of Parker Street, and he couldn't believe that either. His memory served him well, recalling the only other black man in Whiskey Flats, hanged a while back by a bunch of whiskey-soaked rowdies.

Sully McCracken was inspecting a new saddle on the wall of Oscar's store, paying no attention to whatever the man was squinting at.

Doke called him over to the window to show him what he couldn't believe.

Sully, fat and aging, waddled his heavy body over to where Doke was peering out at the street.

"What do you make of that?" Oscar said.

Evincing a modicum of interest, Sully obliged with a glance out the window. "Looks to me like a black man riding a white horse down the middle of Parker Street."

Sully couldn't care less what was taking place outside the door of Doke's hardware. If a man wanted to ride a white horse down Parker Street, there was no law he knew of that said he couldn't do it. Black, blue, red, or white, it didn't matter to Sully.

"Is that all you've got to say?" Oscar said.

"What else can I say? He's a black man riding a white horse down Parker Street."

"We haven't had a colored man around here since they hung Harvey Belt."

"Well, Oscar," McCracken said with an eye on the black man and his white horse, "it 'pears to me we've got ourselves another one."

"Reckon where he came from?"

"Where he came from don't amount to near as much as where he's going."

Oscar took another look out the window and saw the rider dismount in front of the Bang Tail. "Well, I can tell you where he's going," Oscar screeched. "Look at that! He's tying up at the Bang Tail!"

"Damned if he ain't." Sully said.

"You want to go over there?"

"No. You go over there if you want to," Sully said, unable to work up much concern for what made Oscar quiver with curiosity. "What do you want for that saddle?"

"Go ahead and take it," Oscar said, eyes glued to the black man tying his white horse to Eden Fletcher's hitch rail. "We can talk about that later."

Oscar paid no mind to the slender cowboy riding away from the Bang Tail toward the church at the end of the street. Punchers like him came and went by the handful every whipstitch. But he couldn't take his eyes off the black man tying up in front of the saloon that Coldwater just rode away from.

"I'll see you later," McCracken said on his way out, the saddle slung over a shoulder. "That old woman of mine has got more stuff lined up for me to do than it would take a better man an eight-day week to get it done."

Ignoring Sully's departure, Oscar couldn't quit looking to see what the husky dark stranger might do next. What he saw was the black man yanking up the waist of his khaki pants while he looked around, getting his bearings. His blue cotton shirt was dusty and sweat-wrinkled from a long ride on a hot July day.

Sweat salt on the white horse told Oscar the man pushed him hard to get here, from no telling where. He thought it odd a black man would be toting a side arm, but this one's right hip had a revolver mounted on it, sauntering into the Bang Tail like he owned it.

Three minutes later Oscar heard a gunshot from the Bang Tail. He gave his balding head a sorrowful shake. He wasn't surprised something like that would happen to a black man in Whiskey Flats, Kansas, in the summer of 1876

CHAPTER 4

Redford buries the dead

Astride his bay stallion, Redford surveyed the field of sunburnt grass sweeping down to the banks of the Little Big Horn. He was stunned by the silence of death, the sickening waste of life, the residue of one man's ambition to prove himself superior to those he came to kill.

Dismounting, Redford walked slowly among the field of fallen comrades. Respecting Custer's military rank, he buried the colonel on the eastern slope, searching now for the body of his young friend, Cal Courtney. He found Cal with an arrow plunged into this chest. Cal was dead.

Redford knelt beside him and twisted the arrow free, leaving a jagged hole framed in a splash of dried blood. Briefly, he considered taking Cal's body with him back to Kansas. But, it would be a long hard ride from Montana. With no way to protect it on the trail, he decided against it. Instead, he placed Cal's body across his saddle, and carried it up to the eastern ridge above the river. He removed Cal's silver watch and chain, and buried him beside Custer.

He tucked Cal's watch and chain inside his shirt. Back in Whiskey Flats, he'd deliver them to Cal's young widow, Cassie.

He didn't have to guess what Cassie would say. "How come you're not dead?"

He had no answer. To why he survived the slaughter of Little Big Horn he gave little thought, except to be thankful he came away with nothing more serious than a bloody flesh wound.

Leaving behind the battle's devastation, he spurred the bay south. A two-day ride at a comfortable pace brought him into southwestern Wyoming, where he spotted a log barrier surrounding what appeared to be an army outpost.

It was. Visions of a kitchen-cooked meal and a hot bath ambled across his mind. And an even bet that he would come head-to-head with a glassful of the hair of the dog, which men of the west seemed powerless to resist.

Reining the bay that way, he was challenged at the gate of the fort by the duty sergeant. Redford identified himself as a scout from Little Big Horn, and was escorted to the quarters of the post commander, Colonel Adam Brentwell.

The colonel listened to Redford's report of the battle of the Little Big Horn. "What about Colonel

Custer?"

"I buried him," Redford replied. "On the ridge above the river."

"And you marked the grave?"

"I did. With his rifle and hat–" As he would have marked the burial spot of any other dead soldier, including his friend Cal's.

"I see," said Brentwell with a thoughtful nod. "And you were the only survivor?"

"I can't answer that. I don't know."

"I appreciate your report, Redford, and your service. I'll see that both are passed on through proper channels." The colonel paused with a studied look into the face of the survivor of Little Big Horn. "So, what lies ahead for Dan Redford?"

"My scouting days are over. I'm heading home."

"Kansas?"

"Yes, sir," Dan said, "and there's a young lady in Texas I haven't seen for a while."

The colonel smiled as if he understood. "A lady friend?"

"My daughter Ashley."

"A daughter." Fixing him with a questioning gaze, the colonel said, "When did you last see your daughter?"

"It's been about three years now." He could still feel the pain. Every letter she sent ended– I love you, daddy...when will I see you again? But the army was calling, and he had to ride.

"You can tell me it's none of my business, Dan," the colonel said, "but three years is a long time for a young girl to wait for a visit from her father." He laced his thinning gray hair with slender fingers.

"I had a son I hadn't seen for several years. You know the army. If you're not careful, it works its way into a full time job and becomes your whole life. Without your realizing it, after a while everything else fades into the background, and we lose track of time out here."

"Yes, sir."

"I made plans to visit my son in New Mexico, but I waited too long. The week before I was able to take leave, I got word he was shot in a bank holdup–an innocent bystander–killed by an outlaw's bullet. So, take an old man's advice, Dan, and don't wait too long. A life is too short to waste." He cupped Redford's elbow in his right hand and steered him to the door. "The paymaster will have your wages ready tomorrow morning. You'd likely enjoy a hot bath and a good meal."

"I would," Redford said.

"You better take care of that shoulder too."

"Yes, sir."

In the enlisted men's quarters, Redford treated himself to a shave and a half hour in a tub of hot water. He covered the wound in his shoulder with a bandage provided by the post medic.

Joining the troops in the post mess, Redford lit into a plateful of pork roast and fried potatoes, drawing questioning glances from the battle scarred veterans at the table.

"Little Big Horn, was it?" said the man next to him on the left.

With a hot biscuit, Redford swabbed his plate clean of brown beef gravy and gave the man a nod that told him he was right.

"We expected to be called out there," said his neighbor across the table. "The call never came."

From another voice, "Fighting those redskins must have been like hell in a rain barrel."

Cramming his mouth full of gravy-soaked biscuit, Redford's response was a look that told the man he was not eager to talk about the massacre of the Seventh Cavalry.

Sunrise found Redford wrapping his lips around a hot breakfast, after which he drew his wages from the paymaster.

Anxious to hit the trail to Kansas, he gathered up a red bandanna full of biscuits left over from morning mess and dropped them into a saddlebag, along with enough jerky and coffee to get him to Kansas if he was careful. He climbed into the saddle, and pointed the bay's nose south.

Rising from behind the shadowed hills, the sun splashed itself across the length and breadth of Wyoming. Redford gigged the bay into a gentle canter. Kansas was a long ride across rugged country, and time was not his own.

Coldwater goes to church

At the west end of Parker Street, Emitt paused at the door of the little white frame church. He glanced back at the Negro man tying up at the Bang Tail Saloon. Strangers rarely recognized other strangers, but, he thought this one probably was a former slave. In Texas it wasn't uncommon to see a freedman or two, but this was Kansas where

Coldwater suspected a black man was as rare as a mouse at a tomcat picnic. He dismissed it with a shrug, not surprised at anything anymore.

Pastors usually kept close tabs on what was going on in their towns. Coldwater figured Haskell could tell him something that might point him in the right direction in his quest for Dan Redford.

Easing the church door open, he was greeted by a middle-aged man with graying temples and sharp green eyes.

"You're the preacher here?" Coldwater said.

"Yes, sir. How may I be of service to you, young man?"

Haskell was the first and only pastor of the Whiskey Flats Baptist Church. Six years ago, George was dispatched from St. Louis on a preaching mission. It took him only three days to decide the Lord drew him to the right place. He found out early that Whiskey Flats, Kansas, was in bad need of a church, and was going to hell as surely as Moses came down from the mountain with the tablets.

George waged a campaign to raise money, and moral support, for the white-washed frame building that became a monument to his dedication. Struggling to get the steeple built and mounted on the roof, he did it with the help of a half dozen strong backed young disciples. They also installed the stained-glass window near the front door that Haskell ordered from Denver. It took a year to build the church. By the time it was completed, George knew Whiskey Flats was where he belonged.

The home George built for himself and his wife

Hazel was a two-room log house next door to the church. The main room was furnished with a double-sided stone fireplace for cooking and heating. Covering the floor was an oval shaped rug Hazel crocheted from colorful strips of old shirts, dresses, and bed sheets that outlived their usefulness, donated by women of the church. A table and three cane-bottom chairs were arranged in the middle of the rug. In the center of the table stood a lamp with a cloth wick dipped in coal oil. The rough-hewn walls Hazel decorated with embroidered knick-knacks and family photographs.

Since losing Hazel to a battle with pneumonia two winters before, Haskell lived alone. He presided over Hazel's burial, and threw the first and last shovelfuls of dirt on her grave.

George never claimed to be much of a housekeeper, but he kept things as straight and clean as most men would. He recalled Hazel's dislike of clutter as a bane of the devil. Hazel left him with no children, but George loved her dearly.

George petitioned God to assure him he would see Hazel again when it came time to go looking for her. He never told anybody whether God said he would. He believed it any way.

Not many people came to hear him preach at first, so George got by on the proceeds of a pretty skimpy offering plate. He didn't need much. A few dollars for grub and enough to keep the church door open. He made do with the Sunday morning offering, whatever that turned out to be.

No matter how much or how little the offering, George spread it on his kitchen table, counted out ten percent of it, and set it aside "for the poor." That included green beans, ears of corn, and bags of potatoes folks brought when money was scarce. What the churchgoers didn't supply, he depended on the Lord to provide. George would tell you the Lord usually came through.

Haskell stuck out his hand and shook with the young man staring at him from the church's front door. A quick study told him his visitor likely would not be counted among the poor whom George's limited means helped feed and clothe. His visitor needed a shave, and his mop of black hair was thick as a beaver's, as long as a horse's mane. In spite of his roguish appearance, George reckoned his guest probably was a pretty decent fellow.

"I'm looking for a man named Redford," Coldwater said.

"Well, the only man I know by that name is Dan Redford. Is he the one you're looking for?"

"That's right."

"Yes, I know Redford. He's not much of a churchgoer, but he's a good man. The last I knew he was scouting for the army. I understand he was in on that caper of Custer's up at the Little Big Horn a while back."

"Redford was mixed up in that?" Emitt said.

"I expect we can start looking for him to show up back here about any time now. Is he a friend of yours?"

"Only through his daughter."

Coldwater didn't elaborate, and Haskell had no reason to pursue the matter.

Familiar as he was with the ways of youth,

George regarded the young man with a grin. "I've been told you know about whorehouses," Coldwater said. "Any truth to that?"

As if the Lord had just come walking through his front door, causing George to wonder what to do about it, his cheeks turned red, eyes wide with the shock of the young man's unabashed query. Even so, faced with the obligation of responding to such a question, George didn't hesitate. "Only that I encouraged the sheriff to close down the one here in town," he said. "Somebody was getting shot up over there about every other day, so the mayor and Sheriff Whitton agreed to shut it down.

"Some people didn't like it, especially the wranglers, and the drummers who drift in and out from time to time, but it solved the problem. Folks started living longer once it was closed down. Why do you ask?"

Coldwater thought about that for a moment.

"Are you married, reverend?" he asked.

"My wife died two years ago."

"What do you do when–"

"What do I do when what?"

"Well, I mean–you closed the whorehouse down."

"Yes," said the reverend, "I did, didn't I?"

Coldwater smiled to himself as he turned away. Little did he learn about Redford, but he found out something about the preacher.

He left him with a sneaky grin on his face, like the cat that deposited the wriggling snake on the front room floor.

CHAPTER 5

The long ride home

Even with the wondrous tapestry of land and sky, rising and falling like ocean waves as far as his eyes carried him, and the magnificence of snow-covered Rocky Mountain peaks to the west, even in July, Redford's ride from Little Big Horn was lonesome.

Etched on his mind were the silent residue of war and its stench of death, inescapable remnants of the conflict. Redford wouldn't live long enough to forget it.

Echoing off the walls of his memory were the horrified cries of pain, pleas for help that never came for the wounded and dying. Frantic screams of riderless horses, leaping, lunging wild-eyed, crushing with flying hooves the dead and living alike. And the chilling yips and blood curdling war whoops of the tribes, fighting for what the Treaties said belonged to them, what they believed was theirs already, always had been.

Nights under cloudless skies, spectacular displays of brilliant moon and glittering stars, by no means mitigated Redford's relief of putting Little Big Horn behind him. A nightmare of death and dying, a war that served no purpose, costing the cavalry a regiment of dedicated soldiers doing what they were trained to do. He put it behind him, but it would always be a part of him, gnawing at his insides. Asking why? A man born to the saddle, riding alone, took time to get used to.

A wrangler since he was twelve, being alone was part of who he was, but the aloneness still twisted Redford's insides. Dancing across his mind were visions of a hot bath for a body emitting odors resembling those of a bed pan at the old folks home. His nostrils quivered at the thought of a hot meal served on a cloth-covered table. And, always with him rode the tantalizing need for the loving arms of a warm, sweet-smelling woman.

Filing the thought away, he nudged the bay over the rolling grasslands of Wyoming, roamed and hunted for countless generations by the Cheyenne and Pawnee tribes.

Down across cactus and sage brush-infested southwestern Nebraska he rode, making his way into the High Plains of Kansas toward Whiskey Flats. Surviving the slaughter of the Little Big Horn, even the sweltering heat of July, and the monotony of the waterless prairie, took nothing from the good feeling of being back in Kansas.

The open prairie tumbled like angry wind-blown clouds while the sun blistered its way west, searching for shade as scarce as rain. On the banks of streams struggling to stay alive, thirsty roots of cottonwoods and willows sought life-giving moisture. Clumps of Osage orange, requiring less water than other growth, scoffed at the land, thriving where other plants perished for lack of rain.

Prairie dogs scurried for cover. Coiled rattlers announced their blood-curdling presence, shooting shivers of dread up the spines of men who had heard it all their lives, but shrank still from the chilling threat of the rattler. Soaring horse-belly high, pheasants fluttered from the shelter of gray sedge grass. A deer or antelope appeared along the trail, standing statue still from afar with curious, seeking eyes focused on the intruder on horseback. A mama bear, trailed by a ground-sniffing cub, kept a sharp eye on the horseman, resenting his invasion of her territory, challenging him to keep his distance.

From somewhere Redford heard the faint yip-yip of a lone coyote on the hunt for a rabbit or prairie dog for supper. As the sun found a resting place behind the hunkering charcoal hills, the gargled hoot of an owl told him it was time to bed down.

Striking a fire, he set a tin of water on the flame, and tossed into it a double handful of coffee. While it boiled, he unsaddled and rubbed down the sweat-wet bay.

When the roiling bubbles fought their way to the water's surface, he knew the coffee was done. He treated himself to three cups of the steaming black stuff, and chomped down on a stick of beef jerky and a biscuit. The fire, he banked with ashes to keep it alive overnight, discouraging wild creatures from venturing too close.

He stretched out beside the fire, using his saddle for a pillow, and waited for daybreak. Under wide skies clear as a trout stream, stars hung so close Redford thought he might reach out and grab a handful.

An hour before dawn, he was jarred awake by the sound of pounding hoof beats coming from the north. His ears perked up as the sound grew closer and louder. In the cloudless, still moon-splashed night he counted two horses approaching at a hard run.

"Quit your bitchin' about it," he heard a man's gruff voice complain, reining his horse to a halt. To the riders bringing up the rear, he said, "We ain't got another horse, so you'll just have to shut up and make do!"

Redford got to his feet. He eased into the shadows behind the fire where he could see without being seen. There were three of them, two riding double on the trailing horse. The one up behind appeared to be nursing a wounded leg. Gruff Voice was leading the way. Redford figured he was in charge.

"Is that a fire over yonder?" Redford heard one of them say.

"Sure as hell is," the gruff one said.

"Somebody must've rode off and left it burning."

"Damn fool. Could've set the world on fire."

Redford made no move, waiting to find out what

they were up to.

"Anybody there?" he heard somebody say.

"He left his horse too," another said. "Ain't likely a man'd just up and walk away and leave his horse standin' there for the takin'."

"Maybe we had a streak o' luck, Clancy," said the gruff, heavy-chested man on the lead horse. "Move over there and check out that horse."

"Why do I always have to go first?" Clancy whined.

"Because I say so dammit! We need that horse for your brother. He can't ride double plum to Abilene with that busted leg."

"Well, he wouldn't have no busted leg if you hadn't botched up that bank job."

"Just shut up and get the hell over there!"

Clancy, skinny and thin faced, dismounted and moved warily to where Redford's bay was tethered.

"I don't see nobody," Clancy said.

With a cautious look around, he reached for the bay's reins.

"Leave the horse be," Redford said from the shadows.

"What!"

Clancy shivered with fright as if having heard the voice of a ghost. "Bart!" he yelled.

Bart, the gruff, heavy chested one, roared, "Grab that damn horse and let's get the hell outa here!"

"Somebody's here!" Clancy said.

"The hell!" Bart yelled. "You said there wasn't nobody there!"

Bart peered into the darkness, looking for whoever Clancy said was there. He didn't see anybody, but figured Clancy knew what he was talking about. Bart moved closer for a better look. "Look, mister, I don't know who you are," Bart squinting into the shadows, "but we don't want no trouble."

"You've already got more trouble than you can handle if you've got it in mind to steal my horse."

"We got a man here with a bum leg. Caught a hot one at Little Big Horn, and we need a horse for him. That's all we want. Just let us have the horse and we'll be on our way."

"Little Big Horn?" Redford said.

"That's right. We was lucky to get outta there alive."

"What outfit were you in?"

"Richie," Bart called to the younger man with the busted leg riding up behind Clancy. "What outfit was we in?"

Richie wasn't sure. "Whatever Custer was in," he said.

"The Third Cavalry?" Redford said.

"Yeah, that's the one!" Bart said. "The Third Cavalry!"

Redford stepped out of the shadows with his gun aimed at the man called Bart. "Custer was commander of the Seventh Cavalry," he said. "And the Little Big Horn battle was over a week ago."

"Well, I–" Bart flustered. "Maybe I–"

"You've got sixty seconds to clear out of here," Redford said, "and take your friends with you."

"Now, hold on there, we–"

"Thirty seconds."

"Bart!" Clancy yelled.

Bart wheeled about and whipped his horse into a dead run.

Clancy scrambled into the saddle, with Richie still up behind, and took off after Bart.

Redford listened as the sound of hoof beats died away to the west. He holstered his gun and settled down to wait. He knew they'd be back.

A half hour passed before he heard the snap of a dry twig to his right. Richie was wounded. That meant the twig snapper was either Bart or Clancy. The whining Clancy didn't sound like he was itching for a fight, so that left Bart, the one he'd have to deal with.

Redford anticipated their move. He figured they would rush him from both sides at the same time, Bart on his right, Clancy from the left. Dropping back into the shadows, he held his weapon at the ready. His wait was short.

Clancy jumped him from the left with a wild Indian whoop, exposing himself in the light of the fire. Redford planted a slug in his heart, and Clancy plopped to the ground.

Bart came at him from the right. He got within ten feet before he was felled by a blast from Redford's Colt .44.

Redford checked the two lifeless bodies, and found nothing in their clothing that told him who they were. The man called Richie was nowhere in sight, telling Redford he took off when the shooting started.

Sunbeams peeked through the sycamores, turning night into day. Redford wasted no time trying to figure out who the dead men were. It was time to ride.

He kicked out the fire, and dumped the remains of the coffee onto the live coals. He fed the bay a double handful of oats from a saddlebag, anxious to be on the trail before the sweltering sun gobbled up the cool morning breeze. Under a wide blue sky as clear as an unused beer glass, he swung into the saddle. Before the day was noon old the heat would catch up to him.

At mid-morning he paused on top of a grassy knoll, surveying the hazy blue hills huddled together in the west like cattle in a rainstorm. The end of his ride was still a few days away. Saddle-ass weary, he swabbed his sweat-dimpled brow, and swiped the bandanna inside the oily band of his Stetson. He plopped the hat on his head, the brim low in front, almost covering his eyes against the sun's already glaring beams.

He nudged the bay with a heel to the flank, and heard the crack of a rifle off to his left. He rolled off his horse, drew his gun on the way down, and took cover behind a boulder. He scanned the hills, looking for the man whose bullet hissed passed his left cheek.

On the rim of a red dirt cliff, his eyes caught the flashing glint of a rifle barrel pointed in his direction. He slung a shot that way. He saw a man on a black horse wheel around and take off in a hurry.

Redford leaped into the saddle and spurred the bay in pursuit of the shooter. He gigged the bay up the mouth of a draw leading to a level stretch. With leaping strides the bay gained ground on the black.

As he drew closer, he saw the shooter weaving from side to side in the saddle, like he lost control of his mount. The rider tumbled out of the saddle, and hit the sod head first. The black horse kept running, then pulled up, snorted a time or two, and nibbled at the sparse grass.

Skidding to a stop beside the fallen man, Redford slid out of the saddle. The man tried to scramble away, but his wounded leg wouldn't let him.

"Don't shoot!"

Redford could see he was in serious pain. "What the hell are you doing?" Redford asked, holstering his gun.

The man was flat on his back. "You shot my brothers."

He was a cotton-topped youngster about sixteen. His freckles got bigger and redder the harder he gritted his teeth, fighting the pain. Redford glanced around to see if the young man was alone. Satisfied that he was, Redford said, "You must be Richie."

The youngster nodded, gripping his bloody leg.

"How did you get shot up?"

"The bank," Richie said, sobbing. "I didn't want to do it, but Bart made me. He said it took three men to rob a bank."

"Bart was your brother?"

"Him and Clancy. The ones you shot back there."

"So you were going to kill me?"

"I had to try. Look, mister, I'm bad hurt. My leg, it's—"

Redford winced at sight of Richie's left side

from the waist down, saturated with blood. "When did this happen?" he asked.

"Two days ago."

Two days ago! Redford had trouble believing the kid was still alive. "You were robbing a bank?"

"Yeah, it was Bart's idea. Some little town he thought would be easy– Ow!"

"Do you have a last name?"

"Hickley," said the youngster.

Redford knew the name. The Hickley brothers were wanted for bank robbery and cattle rustling in Kansas and Nebraska.

"What's yours?"

"Redford."

The boy's eyes got wide. "Redford? You Dan Redford?"

Redford didn't answer.

"I heard some people talking back there," the boy went on, "about a guy named Redford and– That's how you knew Bart was lying?"

"Yeah. I was in Custer's outfit."

"You were there at– Ouch! You gonna help me or not?"

"I don't spend a lot of time helping people who try to kill me," Redford said. "I'm heading south. If you want to chance it, we might find a doctor some place between here and there."

Richie grimaced his agreement. Redford knew about pain. His wounded shoulder was not healed, and wouldn't be for a while. The bleeding had stopped, though, and the soreness was less severe. The medic at the outpost infirmary gave him some bandages for use on the trail, but Redford declined his offer of a sling. "Can you ride?"

"I don't know–I–"

Redford didn't like the look of it. Gasping for breath, Richie writhed in pain, and likely couldn't sit the saddle. Maybe he could tie the kid in the saddle and lead his horse, Redford thought, but for how long, and how far at a safe gait? "You still thinking about killing me?"

"Maybe later."

"Well, you're in no shape to be killing anybody. You want to see if we can get you up on your horse?"

"Okay. You don't have to do this."

"I know."

"Thanks anyway."

* * * *

Trail's end for Richie

Richie didn't make it through the night. Redford made camp, settled the young man down, trying to make him comfortable. At sunrise, Redford found him dead. He guessed what did the boy in was the loss of blood from the shattered leg. He covered the body with Richie's slicker, and held it in place with a dozen rocks. It wasn't likely anybody would miss the youngster, except maybe his mother, if he had one. She might wonder why Richie didn't show up for breakfast.

Redford mounted up and pointed the bay toward Whiskey Flats.

CHAPTER 6

Hail the hero of Little Big Horn

Like an angry ocean wave, the Kansas prairie tumbled over the High Plains.

A day's ride east of the Colorado border huddled a cow town where a dry tongued drifter once got hold of some bad whiskey. He shot the bartender, and dubbed the town Whiskey Flats. No one knew who the drifter was, but the whiskey got better when the bartender died. Redford walked his bay along the dusty, wagon-rutted road leading into town.

The false-front buildings lining Parker Street didn't look different from the last time he saw them. On the north side of the street stood Bailey's General Store, the tallest building in town right beside the bank. The front of a building with

"Doke's Hardware" painted above the door hunkered across the street, three doors to the right of Eden Fletcher's Bang Tail Saloon.

The other saloon in town was the Deep Six where renegades, rustlers, and ramblers on the run once sought refuge. Sheriff Whitton still nabbed an occasional cow puncher hooting it up like a drunken owl on Saturday night. The hooter got himself deposited in Whitton's jail half way between the Bang Tail and George Haskell's Baptist church.

Polly Payton, Redford remembered, whipped up the best pancakes in the county at her Calico Café, sitting among the cluster of buildings on the south side of the street. His taste buds went to work. He didn't know if Polly was still there, but he had an idea her flap cakes were.

Doc Bowman's office was squeezed between Mrs. O'Rourke's Boarding house and Ben Huskey's barber shop next door to Doke's. Limpy Grogan's livery stable hadn't moved. It still stirred up a stink of horse sweat and fresh manure behind Bailey's. Of course Limpy wasn't there any more since he died of a whiskey-fried liver, marinated from a lifetime of association with Jack Daniel's best.

After Limpy died, his boy Lumpy took over the livery. Lumpy didn't change anything. The stable still emitted the same unsavory essence of sour hay and fresh horse shit.

Fences four rails high stretched around the livestock pens east of town where milling, bawling cattle complained of the sweltering heat. One day the Kansas Pacific Railroad would haul those cattle to slaughter houses in the East where burly, bare-chested men with double-bitted axes would split their heads, skin and gut them. What was left of them would be served as choice cuts of steak, prime rib and roast beef to hungry diners who didn't mind paying more for a steak in Chicago than the steer sold for in Kansas.

At the west end of Parker Street bowed George Haskell's little white church with a wooden cross on top, a symbol of the morality George brought with him from St. Louis. The same morality with which he hoped to convert the town of Whiskey Flats.

Riding past the church, Redford managed a wry grin. He liked George, but never made it inside his church. Not because he didn't believe in God–how else could he escape the threat of the grim reaper at Little Big Horn? Like everybody else in the heat of battle.

Redford confessed to sending up a plea or two. He wasn't sure the Almighty was listening, but something worked in his favor. Even so, believing in God, and talking to Jesus, didn't require his presence to listen to Haskell talk about it on Sunday.

So far, Whiskey Flats showed little inclination to be converted. Haskell kept trying any way, sermonizing Sunday morning and Sunday night, and holding forth at prayer meeting Wednesday evening, or any time someone felt the need for a spiritual refill.

In the one-room school house on the opposite side of the street, Miss Agnes Lethridge held classes every day but Sunday. Miss Agnes was the only teacher the thirteen kids ever had. It was a dread for some parents to think what would happen to their kids if she died. Miss Agnes promised she never would die, but nobody really knew. It could happen any time, and kids in town would be left without a school teacher.

Miss Agnes was sixty-two years old, and never felt around her the arms of a man–that anyone knew of. Of course, there was that time Milo Meeky rescued her from her runaway buggy horse, but nobody counted that–if they even remembered.

Miss Agnes remembered. She nurtured fond memories of the incident, reliving the thrill of being held closer in a man's arms than ever before, or would ever be again.

Milo died in the War fighting on the Confederate side. Miss Agnes never got over that. Never Again would she allow a man to get as close as Milo Meeky.

Whiskey Flats was one of a handful of cattle towns that sprouted like yellow-topped dandelions across the Kansas prairie. It was a part of the feverish migration after the Civil War gave former slaves the courage to desert the South and head west in search of the freedom denied them on the plantations. Whiskey Flats was a welcome oasis for drifters and dry-throated rovers on their way to someplace else.

Drummers sought customers for horse collars, bottles of cheap medicine for just "one tenth of a dollar"–guaranteed to cure all ills. Others touted spittoons, shoe laces, and string ties. They bedded down overnight in Mrs. O'Rourke's boarding house, paid a quarter for a good hot breakfast of steak, eggs over easy, and thin sliced fried potatoes, and washed them down with a pot of steaming black coffee. And, of course, being served by swivel-hipped Lutie Gossage with the bulging bosom provided much of the joy of dining at Mrs. O'Rourke's. After a night's rest, with full stomachs, patrons often climbed aboard the train, or the stage, whichever left town first, headed in the right direction.

For years Whiskey Flats locals looked forward with excitement to the arrival of the Overland Stage, rumbling into places where the iron fingers of the railroad had yet to reach. Now though, the Kansas Pacific tracks extended to Whiskey Flats, providing a new excitement for local citizens to look forward to.

With great anticipation they listened for the hoarse whistle blast and the gasping steam engine of the KP locomotive. Its screeching iron wheels with flying sparks foretold its arrival, pausing for water at the huge tank with its gooseneck west of town. Once filled with water, the engine exhaled a cloud of steam and snail-paced its way out of town.

You never knew who might step off the train when it screeched to a stop at Whiskey Flats, or who might climb aboard when it left. Old timers recalled Buffalo Bill Cody once spent a night at Mrs. O'rourke's boarding house. The next morning he climbed aboard the KP and Whiskey Flats never saw him again.

Dan Redford ambled his bay into town. Whiskey Flats looked mighty good after leaving Little Big Horn behind. He spotted a young woman in the yard of a small frame house surrounded by a white-washed picket fence. Her gingham skirt swirled around her ankles, and her brown hair bounced off her neck as she set a steady gait toward the windmill. A wooden water bucket swung at her side.

Her name was Cassandra Courtney, but most people long since forgot she was ever called anything but Cassie. She was the widow of Cal Courtney, but she didn't know that. Because he was the only who knew what happened at Little Big Horn, Redford would tell Cassie her husband Cal died with a Cheyenne arrow sticking out of his chest.

With a heavy heart Redford approached the young widow, wishing he could bring better news. He wished he could tell her Cal took another way home, and would be showing up any day now. How could he tell Cassie her husband, to whom she was married for only a few weeks before he left for the army, was killed by an airborne missile that didn't know who it hit. And Cal didn't know what struck him down.

What could he say that she would understand? War is war. People kill people they don't know and have nothing against. Soldiers are trained to kill. They get paid thirteen dollars a month and grub for doing it. They also sometimes die. How old or how young they are, or how badly they want the war to be over so they can get back home, spend the rest of their lives with their wives, watching their kids grow up, has nothing to do with whether they live or die.

The army owns them, and they do what the army tells them to do. And sometimes they die.

How could he tell Cassie the lowest he ever felt was the day he buried her husband on a lonely, blood soaked hillside in Montana–a place she'd never seen, and never would see? But the truth must be told.

When she married handsome, dark-haired young Cal Courtney, Cassie was seventeen years old. They grew up together in Whiskey Flats, and Cal was often seen carrying her books home from Miss Agnes's school house.

When they were still quite young, everybody knew Cal and Cassie were "a good fit for the same harness." Cal knew early the fun loving Cassie was the girl he wanted to spend the rest of his life calling her his wife.

When the proper time came, he told Cassie. Though not as certain as Cal, Cassie guessed it would be all right if they got married. She scarcely "had time to catch my breath" before she found herself standing beside Cal down front in the Baptist Church, with half the town of happy, smiling family and friends looking on.

She and Cal said yes to whatever Pastor Haskell said, anxiously waiting for him to say, "I now pronounce you man and wife."

Cal carried his new bride through the front door of the house where he was born. For twenty-four years his parents lived in the same house, built by his father Caleb who died there of the fever three years before.

Seven months later, Cal's mother died in that

house. Nobody knew why. Doc Bowman said it looked like an active woman, who never was sick, "just decided to lie down and die." Her friends suspected she grieved herself into the grave after Caleb was gone.

Cal and Cassie were married only two months, when Cal told Redford he was thinking about joining the army. Cal admired Redford, a friend of his father, and looked to Dan for counsel because he scouted for the U. S. Cavalry.

Redford questioned why a man with a beautiful young bride like Cassie would want to leave her behind so soon, but he kept the thought to himself.

"It's been gnawing at me," Cal confessed.

Redford could tell Cal was a long way from happy with the way things were going in his life. Not about Cassie, whom he dearly loved, but because he wanted to wear the uniform of the U. S. military. Cal needed help making up his mind whether to sign up.

"Well, if you're dead set on getting it done," Redford said, "the Cavalry is the way to go."

"Some of my friends have already gone, and I thought maybe–" Cal said with a shake of his head, and let Redford finish the thought.

"What about Cassie?" He figured Cassie didn't know about it yet, so Cal couldn't answer.

When Cal got around to discussing it with Cassie, she didn't want him to go. In the end, though, she yielded because she knew her young husband wanted to be a soldier. Cal promised he would be back.

Cassie didn't press him for assurance of that. She

didn't know much about military life, but she was pretty sure the army didn't guarantee the safe return of a soldier. She put together a saddlebag full of food and, after a tearful goodbye, sent her husband on his way.

Cal lit out for Fort Riley, and enlisted in a cavalry regiment under the command of Colonel George Armstrong Custer. He hardly arrived before joining the regiment's commitment to ride north to a place called Little Big Horn. He heard somebody say Little Big Horn was in Montana.

Cassie didn't know where Montana was, nor did she know Custer from custard pie. All she cared about was whether he would send her husband home alive.

When the battle was over, the news spread fast as a devil's dance.

Every day Cassie looked for Cal to come riding home. He did not. The longer he stayed away, greater grew Cassie's fear of his being wounded. She tried not to think beyond that. Tossing through sleepless nights, she dared not allow herself to consider that Cal might not come home.

Nearing the windmill, Cassie caught sight of a rider ambling her way. She knew it was Redford. Riding alone. Shading her eyes against the glaring sunlight, she quickened her pace. When Redford came home, she expected Cal to be with him. He wasn't. Her heart was beating so hard she thought it might pop out of her breast. Where was Cal? Was he on his way home? Why wasn't he with Redford?

The bucket shook in her trembling hand. She waited for Redford to pull up beside her. Why was he riding so slowly? Why didn't he kick that horse in the ribs and move faster? When she saw the sorrowful look on Redford's face, Cassie suspected the worst. "Where is he?" The words popped out ahead of hello.

Redford didn't answer. He was struck by the sadness in the eyes of the distraught young woman. He brought Cal's watch and chain from inside his shirt, and handed them to her.

Cassie caressed them with seeking fingers, willing, by fondling what once belonged to her husband, by some magical means she could bring him back unscathed by the ravages of war.

"Where is he?" she screamed again, bursting into tears. "He joined the cavalry because of you!" She began flailed away at Redford with the empty water bucket. "Where is my husband?"

Redford slid out of the saddle and grabbed her by the shoulders. He drew her close, trying to console her. She would not be consoled. She flung the bucket aside, and pounded his chest with both fists.

Redford freed himself, climbed back into the saddle, and rode away without a backward glance. Whatever else he might say to Cassie would be wrong.

Her mind was made up, and talking wouldn't change it. "How come you're not dead?" she flung at his departing back.

CHAPTER 7

Happy Fourth of July

Observance of the one-hundredth anniversary of the Declaration of Independence emptied the countryside. Celebrants swarmed into Whiskey Flats. Buckboards, one-horse buggies, flatbeds, springboard wagons, and saddle mounts, lined both sides of Parker Street. The festivities started at ten o'clock in the morning, and many of the younger participants didn't finish celebrating until after ten o'clock that night.

The Stars and Stripes fluttered on temporary poles mounted on store fronts.

Fat Mayor Clarence Stokes rounded up a "marching band" of a bugler left over from the Civil War, a fife player who was short of breath, a young school boy with a banjo who took three lessons from a traveling musician, and a one-armed veteran with a drum.

From miles around farmers and ranchers with families, and hired hands anxious to belly up to the bar, crowded Parker Street elbow-to-elbow to applaud the parade.

On a wooden platform erected for the occasion in front of the Mercantile, elderly, blue-haired Ethel Storm from the Baptist Church choir sang "The Battle Hymn of the Republic" in a quavering contralto, straining a bit to reach the high notes of the "glory hallelujahs."

Preacher Haskell opened the festivities with a prayer ending with "gratitude and hope for the future of our great country, through our eternal God, amen."

The mayor droned through a sixty-seven minute tirade, reminding some of his bored constituents of someplace else they were supposed to be. Many of them went looking for it, and wound up waiting in line at the lemonade stand.

The ladies' circle from the church set up a tent for serving hot fudge, pork chops, or steak with green beans, and mashed potatoes smothered with cream gravy, all for a quarter a plate. The food was set out on rough pine planks stretched across saw horses covered with red, white and blue-checkered cloths.

Beulie Baucum's special recipe banana pudding was the most popular dessert. Served with a wooden ladle from a wash tub, the pudding went fast, since it never before passed the lips most of the young folks. Chocolate cakes accompanied a colorful assortment of pie slices going for a nickel apiece, prepared by the best cooks in the county. The proceeds were earmarked for the purchase of new hymn books for George Haskell's church.

The Fourth of July fell on a Wednesday, not a good day for the men who worked cattle and crops, whose absence would reduce the size of the crowd. So, the mayor asserted his authority as the town's only elected official, and proclaimed the festivities be set back three days. Independence Day of 1876, therefore, was observed in Whiskey Flats, Kansas, on Saturday the seventh day of July, "where it ought to be anyhow," since Saturday was when farm and ranch people came to town to do their shopping.

The women spent time at the Mercantile buying needles, thread, and material for new summer dresses and slat sunbonnets. They gathered in the back room of the Bang Tail Saloon for Eden Fletcher's tea and sugar cookies, where no man was welcome.

The young folks–barefoot boys in blue bib overalls and straw hats–kicked the can, or played hide-and-seek, with romping dogs chasing after them, giving away their hiding places. The girls, in ankle length dresses and high topped shoes, played hopscotch and jumped rope, chatting with friends they hadn't seen for a while. All looked forward to Billy Whomper's annual fireworks display at sundown in the middle of Parker Street.

Some of the men pitched horseshoes or played croquet. The checker championship used up a good deal of time at the Bang Tail's gambling tables. Horace Copeland finally won the prize again–a brand new checker board from Sears & Roebuck's summer catalog. Others dickered with Oscar Doke for hardware supplies, new harness, and rolls of barbed wire for repairing sagging fences.

The limp, whiskey-laden bodies of several of the younger men who took advantage of the celebration to "rassle the tiger" were hauled out from the saloons by friends who dumped them into wagons. Some were tied in their saddles, the mounts trusted to find their way home.

Half a dozen rowdies, rounded up by Sheriff Whitton for disturbing the peace, spent the night in his jail. More would have been nabbed, but the jail wasn't big enough to hold them. The next morning, Whitton turned them loose, all hung over and stumbling from a night of reveling.

The annals of Whiskey Flats, revealed no record of how many of the celebrants darkened the door of George's church Sunday morning.

In Ben Huskey's barber shop the wooden benches circling the walls were lined ass-to-ass with men waiting their turn for haircuts. Their wait was filled with conversation about what happened since the last time they talked about it. Some even paid Ben two bits for a shave while they napped in his chair, a rare luxury, since most of them did their own shaving, except on Independence Day. They couldn't have done it without the help of their wives, whom they instructed, "Woman, come shave my neck."

And, of course, the battle of the Little Big Horn was chewed on as the major event of the time. Huskey's barber shop was rife with opinions of what took place up there.

"Looks to me like Custer got what was comin' to him," said Joe Fraley.

"Dumb bastard!" Chick Cummins put in. "Thought he was gonna blow in up there and ride roughshod over them redskins and put 'em all six foot under."

"Well, now just hold on there, Chick," Bob Crews said.

Bob quit farming at eighty-seven because an oak tree he was chopping down with a double-bitted axe fell on his left shoulder and drove the ankle bone through his foot. Doctors tried to save the foot, but finally yielded to the demands of the crusty old farmer.

"Hell, give me something I can walk on so I can get back to work," Crews told them. With a leather strap they bound a piece of wood to the stub of his left knee, and Bob went back to work. He soon learned walking behind a plow was harder with one good foot.

Bob felt the need to hold his younger friends in check. Without a moment of hesitation, he went to work on that. "Well now, we wasn't there," Bob said, "so we've got no way of knowing how that Little Big Horn thing come off."

"I know if he had used his head," Cummins countered, "common sense would've told him he ain't gonna kill no six thousand bumble-bee-mad Injuns with a handful of soldiers on horses."

"Wasn't six thousand," Fraley said. "It was four."

Crews put in, "Lots of folks have a frightful

shortage of common sense anymore."

"I've heard talk," said bewhiskered Ellis Blue with the sunken eyes, "there wasn't but one man come out of Little Big Horn alive."

"Redford," Fraley said.

"Dan Redford?" Crews said.

"Reckon how he got out?" Petey Wilks wanted to know, holding a hand to his ear so he could hear the answer.

Nobody had one.

Chick Cummins was a hawk-nosed sixty-three-year-old with a sharp chin. He stuck it out. "Ask me," Chick said, shaking a fist to emphasize his words, "I'd say that Redford fella was a dad-blamed hee-ro. Anybody with one eye and half sense knows there wasn't no way Custer was gonna come out ahead of them riled-up Injuns, no matter how many men he took up there and throwed at 'em."

"Ain't nobody knows what took place up there," was Linus Windsor's quiet contribution, "'less it's Redford, and we ain't heard from him yet."

"May not either," Crews put in. "No telling where he is now."

The bald headed barber, lean and stooped from a lifetime of bending over heads of shaggy hair, snipped away at Fess Beeber's gray head. Snoring in Huskey's chair with his face under a hot wet towel, Fess made no contribution to the discussion.

Huskey did a lot of listening during the Little Big Horn debate, agreeing with some comments, scoffing at others.

He decided it was time to put a cap on it before it got out of hand. "I don't know who's right, and I don't know who's wrong," Ben said with a grin, "but I've got a free shave and haircut for the first man that shuts up about it."

Charley Greer, a wizened little old non-participant with shaggy sideburns, was the only man on the bench who didn't open his mouth to voice an opinion about what happened at Little Big Horn.

Charley was awarded the free shave and haircut. Everybody scoffed at Charley, gave him good natured slaps on the back, and laughed out loud.

Nothing was settled regarding the success or failure of Little Big Horn. The only man who knew was on his way to Whiskey Flats.

CHAPTER 8

Back home again

Redford was on the trail from Little Big Horn on the 7th of July. The celebration of the Declaration of Independence in Whiskey Flats didn't miss him. While the mayor's long-winded speech was putting his audience to sleep, Redford was riding south from Montana. It was two days after the last firecracker fizzled, and the bars were wiped clean of whiskey drippings when he rode in.

Red, white and blue banners still hugged the posts along the boardwalk. They brought a faint smile to his lips. The pages of his memory fluttered back to another celebration in another place at another time .... no, Danny...you're drunk...maybe...we shouldn't be doing this...you want to quit?

He filed the recollection away in a private corner of his mind, but he'd get back to it. He always did.

Mayor Stokes called for volunteers to clean up the rubble left from the July Seventh festivities, but got no takers. Farmers had cows to milk and hogs to slop. Ranchers always had more to do with their cattle herds than they had time to get done. Some of them pleaded with apologetic looks on their faces: They shouldn't have taken the time to come to town for the celebration in the first place.

The rolls of blubber around the mayor's middle prevented his bending over far enough to pick up the clutter on Parker Street. In the end, even he begged off, citing a sudden rheumatic setback.

Redford was greeted by tattered red-white-and-blue banners, discarded napkins, and spent firecracker shells. Nudging his bay down Parker Street, the sinking sun at his back, he looked like a shadow on horseback.

The mayor was the first to hail Redford as he rode by.

"Is that you, Redford?" Stokes called, squinting from his front porch rocking chair.

Redford, still mulling over his encounter with Cassie Courtney, heard the mayor call, but had other things on his mind.

Cal asked him to look after Cassie if he didn't make it back, and Redford said he would. Cassie acted like she couldn't care one way or the other what Redford said, giving him no chance to explain his obligation to her dead husband.

With a casual wave and half a smile, Redford returned the mayor's greeting and kept moving.

To his front door, the mayor yelled over his shoulder, "Martha, come 'ere!"

Redford gigged the bay along Parker Street, and pulled up in front of the building with a "Sheriff's Office" slab of oak nailed above the door. He dropped a rein over the rail, pushed open the door, and stepped inside.

The man behind the desk said, "Great God a'mighty! Is that you, Redford?"

"Hello, Demp."

Bouncing up out of his chair, Demp Whitton took three giant steps toward Redford, and stuck out his hand. Redford shook it with a hardy grip.

"All bright eyed and bushy tailed," Whitton said with a broad grin. "How the hell did you get out of that place alive?"

Redford traded him grin for grin, and said, "I wasn't ready to die."

"Sit down, man, and take the load off."

"We can visit later, Demp. I just thought you ought to know– Does the name Hickley mean anything to you?"

"Hickley? Why do you ask?"

"Three brothers, Bart, Clancy, and Richie. I shot two of them, and watched the other one die.

They jumped me up north, and tried to steal my horse. I heard them say something about a bank they tried to rob."

"Tried to rob?"

"From what the boy said, they didn't make it. The youngest, Richie, was shot up pretty bad. I tried to help him, but he died on the trail."

Whitton pulled open a desk drawer, and brought

out a handful of wanted fliers. "If they're who I think they are," he said, flipping through the fliers. "Yep! Here it is. Hickley brothers, wanted for bank robbery in Nebraska and Kansas, believed to be– Well, I'll be damned! And you shot these hombres? How did it happen?"

"Like I said, Richie was shot up. His brothers wanted my horse to give him something to ride, and that's when the trouble started.

"I figured you should know. If you've been looking for them, you can quit looking."

"I'll be damned," Whitton said again. "There's a $500 reward, you know."

"Give it to George. He probably could use some new Bibles."

"All right. I'll make a full report of this, Dan," Demp said. "The county prosecutor will be glad to hear it."

Again he put out his hand and Redford took it in a friendly shake. "Welcome back, Dan. It's good to see you. Come around when you get time and we'll have a cup of coffee and catch up."

"I will," Redford said on his way out.

"And, Dan–"

"Yeah, Demp?"

"That badge is still here in my drawer any time you want to pin it on again."

"I'll think about it."

Mounting up, Redford rode east along Parker Street.

He reined the bay to in front of the Bang Tail Saloon, and dropped a rein over the hitch rack. He slapped the trail dust from his shirt and pants, and stretched the weariness out of his leathery six-foot-three frame.

He stomped his boots free of dust, adjusted his gun belt with its silver buckle lined with cartridges for the Colt .44 riding his hip. Habit prompted him to take a sweeping glance along the street, up one side and back on the other.

Nothing unusual about the horses and wagons lined up on both sides–except for the sleek white horse standing next to where he tethered his bay. A horse as fine as that was a rare sight; beside the blacks and bays in northwest Kansas. Wondering who the white horse belonged to, Redford gave his head a curious shake and strolled into the Bang Tail.

With a bright smile, Eden Fletcher greeted him from behind the bar.

"Howdy, cowboy," she said. "I thought you might be moseying back down this way. What can I get you?"

"What have you got?"

She responded with a sideways grin. "Anything you haven't had lately?" She set out a glass and poured it full of whiskey. "I hear you had a rough ride."

"You heard right," Redford said.

He up-ended the glass, and spotted a black man sitting alone at a table in the corner, nursing a cup of coffee.

"Who's the man in the corner?" Redford said to Eden.

"I don't know," Eden said, "but he just cleaned out a passel of ugly, and shot one of the Covington boys."

"Which one?"

"The youngest, Cecil. One of those young punks who thinks he can out shoot any gun alive."

"Did he kill him?"

"No, nothing serious, but it got Cecil's attention."

"What happened?"

"When the stranger came in, Cecil smarted off to me about letting garbage like that stink up the place. The black man paid him no mind till Cecil made a grab for his arm. The black man shoved him away, and Cecil went for his gun."

"And?"

"He shot the gun out of Cecil's hand.

"Cecil's brother didn't make a move, except to get him out of here."

"Which brother?"

"Nathan. But that's not all of it," she said. "The black man wiped out Rance Gomer too."

Eden told him how the Negro ambled into the Bang Tail Saloon as casually as if he had done it every day of his life. Young Cecil Covington spotted him right away, scowling when the black man pulled up at the bar.

Eden had seen previous displays of Cecil's cocky nature. She slid him a warning glance that told him to behave himself. Cecil ignored it.

Eden greeted the black man with a friendly smile, and he responded with a nod.

"What would you like?" Eden said.

"Coffee," he said.

His name was Thomas Belt. His deep wearisome sigh let Eden know he rode a long way, and it took a long time to get to the bar in her saloon.

Eden wondered how long, and from how far, but didn't ask. She figured if she needed to know, he'd tell her.

Most strangers who made it into her place after such a ride would kill for a glass of whiskey. This one ordered coffee.

"Cream and sugar?" Eden said.

"Black," he said, "and a kind word would be nice."

"We can handle that," she said. "We've got a good supply of both."

She set a cup out for him and poured it full from a black bottomed coffee pot.

He thanked her, and tipped the cup to his lips.

"We don't get many people like you in here," Eden said.

Before he could respond, the newcomer heard a sneering voice behind him. "There's a damn good reason for that."

It was the Covington boy. He was nineteen years old going on dumb. Cecil had a bent for poking his nose in matters that were none of his business, often with unpleasant consequences.

And, it appeared to Eden, he was at it again.

Belt moved his head for half a look into the face of the young man with a crooked mouth, and a headful of tousled brown hair sticking out from under his hat. A dozen or so card palmers at the poker tables, hearing the voices, swiveled their necks to watch.

"I'm surprised at you, Eden," Cecil said, "letting garbage like this come in here and stink up the place."

"Let it go, Cecil," Eden said. "I'll take care of this."

"If you don't, I will."

Cecil's mild mannered older brother Nathan placed a hand on his shoulder. "Let's go, Cecil," he said.

Cecil shook it off, adjusting the holster on his right hip. To Belt, he said, "You wanna walk out, or be carried out feet first?"

Belt sipped at his coffee.

"You better be looking at me, boy, when I'm talking to you!" Cecil yelled with a threatening swat at Belt's arm.

Thomas Belt stood a head taller than Cecil, and weighed two-hundred-forty-four pounds, dwarfing the slightly built younger man.

When Cecil slapped at his arm, Belt gave him a shove that sent Cecil sprawling on his backside. Cecil went for his gun, and Belt fired a shot that creased the wrist on Cecil's gun hand. The gun dropped and skittered across the wooden floor.

Cecil grabbed his bleeding right hand with a stunned look on his face, reflecting disbelief that he was bested by a black man.

"You know this boy?" Belt said to Nathan.

"He's my brother."

"You better get him home," Belt said. "His mama's probably worried sick about him."

"His mama's dead," Nathan said.

Thomas pinned him with a solemn look. He knew what it was like to have a dead mama. After the Civil War, Thomas served seven years of a life sentence in a Mississippi prison for beating the life out of a former plantation field boss with his own shovel. The field boss, Bozo Cliff, one day whipped Thomas's father Harvey with a leather thong when Harvey was so sick he couldn't stay on his feet.

Weak though he was, Harvey crawled out of bed that morning and answered the call to join the crew heading for the cotton fields. By mid-morning Harvey could no longer walk, and collapsed into his cotton basket.

Cliff lashed Harvey with the leather thong, and screamed, "You lazy lout! Get up from there and get back to work!"

Harvey, lying prostrate between cotton rows, wrapped his arms around his head to protect himself from further blows. Twelve-year-old Thomas watched, horrified. Shaking with anger, a slave on Felix Minwell's Mississippi plantation, he could do nothing to avenge his father's cruel treatment. But he promised himself that he would one day see Cliff again, and find a way to pay him back for the brutal lashing of his father.

He found him.

In the seventh year of Thomas's imprisonment, an earth tremor shook the ancient stone prison and reduced it to shambles. The armed guards ran for cover, and Thomas ran to freedom. Racing through fields of cotton, indigo, and tobacco, splashing across streams, Thomas kept running, praying that he would outrun the bloodhounds and bulldozers.

Lungs ready to burst, he dared not stop to rest, forcing himself to keep going, thinking only of reaching his mother before she died. Her last letter told him she likely would not live long enough to see him again. He got there in time, but a few days later she died.

Nathan led his little brother out of the Bang Tail with his bleeding hand wrapped in a red bandanna.

Thinking the matter was settled, Thomas turned back to his coffee at the bar.

The poker players thought so too, and again cupped their cards in calloused hands.

But Rance Gomer, a flabby, long haired bully with a thin, raspy voice and tobacco stained teeth, hadn't seen enough. Flanked by a couple of smirking cronies, Googoo Pry and Henny Eckles, Gomer observed the fracas between Cecil and Thomas.

Nathan led Cecil away, and Gomer said to Belt, "Hey, boy."

Growing up in the fields of Master Minwell's plantation, many times was Thomas Belt called "boy." He didn't like it then, and he had no plans for putting up with it now.

"You done good against that kid," Gomer taunted.

Gomer had a bent for finding trouble where most people wouldn't look for it. He was a Covington wrangler who never showed up in town without those two plug uglies, Pry and Eckles, with guns strapped to their thighs.

"Mostly we string up black boys around here," Gomer snickered, joined by Pry and Eckles. "Reckon how you'd do against a man?"

Belt turned his head half way and caught a piece of Gomer's jeering face in the corner of his eye. No need to waste time responding to this ruffian's taunts.

"What's the matter, boy?" Gomer jeered. "Cat got your tongue?"

Belt moved his body far enough to the left to aim a steady gaze that came to rest on the face of the smirking Rance Gomer.

Thomas said, "Have you got a cat?"

"What?"

"Have you got a cat?"

"What the hell?"

"I just wondered how he'd like your tongue if I fed it to him."

Gomer bounced to his feet, kicked his chair backwards, upended the poker table, and made a token move toward his gun, but stopped short of drawing.

"You black son of a bitch!" he screamed. "You take that back!"

Thomas never blinked. "Call off your dogs and we'll see what kind of man you are."

Gomer waved a hand at Googoo and Henny, letting them know he didn't need any help taking care of the black man. Gomer made a headlong dive that Belt sidestepped, and Gomer collided headfirst with the bar.

Belt dragged him to his feet and clobbered him with a right fist to the jaw that sent him reeling against the overturned table. Glazed eyed, Gomer staggered to his feet. Belt met him half way. Gomer's left-handed uppercut went wild, and Belt floored him with a solid right to the face. Pry and Eckles went for their guns.

"Hold it right there." Googoo and Henny stared into the muzzle of a double-barreled shotgun in the hands of Eden aimed at them across the bar. "Make a move and I'll kill you," she said.

The two hard cases believed she would. They backed off with a scowl.

Thomas grabbed Gomer by the collar, dragged him to the batwings, and shoved him out onto the boardwalk.

Gomer plopped down like a bag of potatoes. He pulled his heavy body to his feet, and wobbled away with choking coughs, hands at his throat.

"You two clear out," Eden ordered Pry and Eckles with the shotgun leveled at their belt buckles. "You better make yourselves scarce around here." She shook off their vengeful stares, lifted the gun level with their eyeballs, and fingered the trigger.

The two toughs slunk away, headed for the door.

"That's how it went," she said to Redford. "The black man never worked up a sweat."

"Would you have shot them?" Redford said.

"Damn right. This is my place, and I'll clean it out any time it needs it."

Redford admired her spunk. He grabbed the bottle and glass, and carried them to the table in the corner."Mind if I join you?" he asked to Belt.

Belt motioned him to a chair. "I'm not very good company right now."

"How's that?"

"Bloodshed makes me sick to my stomach."

Redford grinned, threw a leg over the back of the chair, and sat down. "I'm Dan Redford." He put out his hand, and Belt shook it.

"Thomas Belt."

Redford poured some whiskey in his glass, and tilted the bottle toward the stranger.

"No, thanks," Belt said. "I get mean when I drink."

"Where are you from?"

"No place you'd recognize."

"Do you know whose blood you just shed?"

"If you mean do I know his name, no I don't. But assholes don't take a long time to get noticed."

Redford nodded his agreement.

"You just wiped out a couple of them," he said. "Rance Gomer. Cecil is the boy you shot, the son of Jonas Covington."

"Sounds like somebody big."

"Well, he is. You need to know you shot the son of the biggest rancher in the county."

"He brought it on himself. I didn't come here looking for trouble."

"What did you come for?"

Over the rim of his cup, Belt sipped at his coffee with a steady gaze at Redford. How much could he afford to tell this man sitting across the table from him? They just met, traded names and handshakes. Strangers facing each other, each with questions about the man he was looking at.

Redford waited for a response to his question.

Belt decided he needed to confide in somebody, and Redford looked like a man he could trust. He might know something of Harvey's whereabouts. "I'm looking for my father," Thomas said. "Harvey Belt. I was told he headed this way."

Redford shook his head. He knew nothing of his father. "I've been away in the army," he said.

Belt held up his coffee cup in Eden's direction. She brought the pot and refilled it.

"Little Big Horn, wasn't it?" Belt asked after Eden moved away.

"How would you know that?"

"If only one man rides away from a war, word gets around. People want to know who he is.

Some people think you ran scared."

"Is that so?"

"Other people think you're a hero because you got out alive."

"What do you think, Mr. Belt?"

"I take a man for what I see, not for what somebody tells me."

Redford gave him an appreciative nod. "Covington will be coming," he said.

"I figured he would be," Belt said, "even before I knew who he was."

"He won't be alone."

Belt's answer was a 'whatever' shrug.

"A big man needs big guns to cover his backside." Redford got up to leave, again offering Belt the bottle.

He shook his head no.

"In your place," Redford said, "I'd make myself scarce."

"Thanks for the advice. But if I leave, it won't be because they scared me off."

"How did you learn to shoot like that?"

"Coyotes and rattlesnakes."

"Coyotes and rattlesnakes don't shoot back,"

Redford said with a grin. "You might want to sharpen your aim some, if you're planning to be around here long. Aim for the chest. It's the biggest target."

"I'll work on that."

"What about Gomer?" Redford said.

"Gomer?"

"The man you threw out of here. He's a Covington hand."

Belt offered a weary smile and shook his head. "The woods are full of them," he said.

"You bit off a pretty tough chew."

"I have strong teeth."

Meeting his gaze, Redford showed appreciation for the honest, straightforward man, sipping at a cup of black coffee, minding his own business. He was likely bound for more trouble than bagging a bushel of raccoons. All Belt wanted was to locate his father, but he probably stirred up more trouble than he could handle.

"You'll need them," Redford said of Belt's strong teeth.

He strode back to the bar and slid some coins toward Eden.

"What did you find out?" she asked.

"His name is Thomas Belt. He's looking for his father, Harvey."

She locked her eyes on his. She'd heard talk about a man named Harvey Belt, the one they lynched a couple of months back. That was the day she took the buckboard to Dodge City for supplies and stayed overnight. When she got back the next day, Jake told her about the hanging. Since then, she'd heard no mention of the incident.

"Harvey Belt," she said, as if to herself. *Does Redford know about the hanging? Since he wasn't involved, does it matter?*

"And this Thomas Belt is Harvey's son?" she asked.

"That's what he said. Well–" He turned to go.

"Are you leaving?" Eden said.

"I've got to find a place to bed down for the night."

With a slow grin, she said, "I've got a place upstairs."

"How much?"

"No charge for the hero of Little Big Horn."

He glanced over his shoulder.

"Are you expecting someone else?" he asked.

Eden answered with a provocative stare from the tops of her smoky eyes.

She needed to tell Redford about the man who said he was going to kill him, but he hadn't done it yet, so that could wait.

"I bet it's been a while since you slept in a good woman's bed," she said.

Cautious as a rabbit at a coyote convention in case he read her wrong, Redford aimed a questioning gaze into her gold flecked eyeballs. He decided she was inviting him to share what a quick calculation told him was her featherbed with soft white sheets and a goose down pillow. The kind of thing a trail weary man spends a lot of time thinking about.

"I'll just get my stuff," he said.

"I've got all the stuff you'll need," she said.

"How about a bath?"

"I've got one of those. It's just right for a weary traveler."

CHAPTER 9

Meet Jonas Covington

Covington was a hard-nosed taskmaster who never let the sun get up before he did. Breakfast was whatever his Cree squaw housekeeper put on the table. He took time to eat only because it sustained his bulky body for the day's work ahead. That behind him he saddled up and worked himself out of daylight, quitting only when darkness drove him in. Jonas pressed his sons to work as hard as he did, and every fall they drove thousands of cattle to the Kansas Pacific railhead for shipment to the East.

The best grazing land in the county belonged to Jonas Covington. Settlers who wanted to run their stock on his grass, water them at his stream, and build fences around his open range, were denied access. If they tried to invade his territory, he met them with armed resistance. His life was working the claim staked out forty years before by his father who fought Indians, grasshopper infestation, suffered bone-chilling winters, and summers so hot bare feet blistered, and a man could hardly breathe.

Over the years, Jonas expanded his range to include more acres than any other rancher in northwest Kansas. It would take a man on a good horse all summer to ride around what Jonas claimed as his Circle C ranch.

The saddest day of Jonas's life was when he lost his wife Cora after a long bout with pneumonia in the winter of '71. She left him three sons. Good men all.

If there was a flaw in his pride, it was his youngest son, Cecil. Since he turned thirteen, Cecil went around picking fights with total strangers, some kind of scrape from which he had to be rescued. Now going on twenty, a sound thrashing with the buckle end of his father's leather belt was still not uncommon for Cecil as punishment for "pulling some dumb ass stunt."

Jonas's oldest boy, Jubal, was five years old when he fell out of a wagon and a rear wheel ran over his head. It took twenty stitches for Doc Bowman to close the wound. Because of the injury, Jubal, now almost thirty, was left mentally weak. Jubal followed his father around like a speckled pup, waiting to be told what to do. Six-feet-five inches tall, Jubal's bulky body tipped the scales at around three hundred pounds. He was innocent as a newborn calf, but homesteaders cringed at sight of Jubal's witless grin and imposing hulk. Just the sight of him caused some to change their minds about where they wanted to graze and water their livestock.

Nathan, Jonas's middle son, was a mild-mannered young man who never gave his father a moment's worry. Nathan was always where he was supposed to be when he was supposed to be there. What his father told him to do, Nathan did, without question nor complaint. Quiet and intelligent, saying little except what needed to be said, everybody knew when Nathan told them something, they could count on its being the way he said.

Any time Jonas saw Demp Whitton riding out to the Circle C, he stewed in the saddle. More often than not, the sheriff was on his way to tell him something he didn't want to hear–such as a fracas his youngest got himself into.

It was not Whitton Jonas saw galloping in his direction as Jonas sat his roan stallion scanning his herd for newborn calves. It was Nathan. Cecil, aboard his paint mare, was trailing his brother, his right hand wrapped in a blood soaked bandanna.

Jonas gave his head an aggravated shake, unleashed a barrage of obscenities, and wondered what kind of mess Cecil was involved in this time.

"Pa," Nathan said, pulling up beside his father, "Cecil got shot."

"Shot?" Jonas said. "Who the hell shot him?"

"There was a black man–"

"My boy got shot by a black man?"

"I have to tell you, Pa, Cecil started it."

"You mean to tell me your brother got shot by some slave?"

"He's not a slave, Pa, he's–"

To Cecil, Jonas roared, "You let a black man shoot you, and you never shot back?"

Cecil hung his head and said nothing.

"Answer me, boy!" Jonas demanded. "You let a black man beat you?"

"I guess so."

"You guess so! Let me see that hand." Cecil unwrapped the bandanna, exposing a red slash on his right wrist. Jonas turned the hand over a time or two, inspecting the damage. "You're not hurt bad," he scowled. "Can you pull that trigger?"

Cecil wiggled his trigger finger a time or two, and nodded. "I think so," he said weakly.

"You get back in there!" Jonas shouted.

He ripped off his belt and used the buckle end to pummel Cecil's backside. Cecil's face contorted in pain. "Remember who you are, boy," Jonas screamed. "Us Covingtons don't tuck tail and run from a fight."

"Pa," Nathan said, "the man never–"

"Did you hear me, boy?" Jonas yelled at Cecil, ignoring Nathan. "I don't want to see you back out here till it's done. You hear me, boy?"

"Yes, sir," Cecil said.

With a hang dog look Cecil put a spur to his mare's flank and reined her toward town.

Casting his father a vengeful stare, Nathan watched his slinking little brother ride away toward town.

Jonas kept an eye on Cecil to be sure he headed in the right direction.

Jubal flashed a foolish grin.

CHAPTER 10

Eden looks back

Watching Redford stuff his shirt tail in, Eden drew the bed sheet up to her chin.

She didn't want to think about it, but at times like this she couldn't not think about it. Times when men invited her to supper, for a drink, a ride in the country, or even for an innocent cup of coffee, after watching her dance half naked on the stage of the Playhouse Casino.

How many were there been? How many didn't matter since she wasn't permitted to accept any of their invitations.

Jack Claxton told her all they wanted was to "get in her pants."

Claxton was the part of her life she wished she could forget.

Eden's father Clement died from a ruptured appendix when she was twelve. After the funeral, her mother Angela sent Eden's younger brother and sister to live with their grandmother. Angela's mother agreed to take them into her home because her daughter couldn't afford to feed and clothe three children.

Her husband buried, Angela relinquished responsibility for her two younger children. She took scissors to her waist length brown hair, and shortened her name to the more flamboyant Angie. Flaunting her newborn freedom, she cast off the yoke of obligation, and went in search of what she heard friends call "a fun time."

She took to going out late at night, leaving Eden alone, sometimes until the wee hours of morning. In no uncertain terms, she instructed her twelve-year-old daughter– "Do not answer the door," because she didn't want the neighbors to know she was leaving Eden alone.

In the saloons and gambling halls of Kansas City, Angie found what she called an "escape from boredom." She frequently went dancing and drinking, sometimes with friends, often with total strangers, some of whom Eden found in her mother's bed the next morning.

Many times her mother didn't come home after a night of doing the town.

One night while Angie was away, Eden fell asleep reading a favorite book by the light of the coal oil lamp on a bedside table. Sometime in the night she accidentally struck the lamp with her hand. The lamp tumbled off the table, splashing oil and flames across the wooden floor. The room filled with smoke and flames before the half awake Eden realized what was happening. She made a frantic effort to find her way out, but she stumbled over a chair and fell to the floor.

Trying to escape the burning house, she heard the excited chatter of neighbors gathered outside. She wanted to call to them but dared not because her mother's stern warning not to answer the door still rang in her ears.

Still, bordering on hysteria, Eden opened her mouth to call out to the neighbors, but panic silenced her voice. Beside herself with fright, blinded by smoke and flames, she flattened out on her stomach and started crawling toward where she thought the door would be.

She heard the crash of shattering glass, and a man's voice called, "Over here, over here!"

On blistered hands and knees, Eden worked her way toward the sound of the voice. Finally she reached the front room. Someone threw a brick through a window, and a man reached in and helped her out through the shard-framed opening. She didn't know whether he was the same man who called to her, but it didn't matter. Any kindness was welcome. Once clear of the fire ravaged house, Eden collapsed in his arms.

Neighbors fussed over her, saying nice things, checking the seriousness of her burns, trying to console the frightened, weeping young girl sobbing out of control.

The man who carried her to safety was Jack Claxton. Her mother never came home.

Eden wasn't ready for Redford to know about that. Not yet any way. But there was something she needed to tell him.

"Some stranger was in my place looking for you," she said.

"Did he say what he wanted?"

"He said he had some business to take care of with you."

"What kind of business?" Redford wanted to know.

"He said he was going to kill you."

Redford gave her a sharp look, buckled on his gun belt and grabbed up his hat. "Who was he?"

"He didn't say, and I didn't ask," Eden said." I just wanted him out of my place."

"Was he old, young—what?"

"Young. Maybe twenty. Maybe younger. It's not always easy to tell."

"What did he look like?" Redford said.

"Pretty ordinary, like most of the punchers who come in here."

A young punk most likely, Redford thought, looking for a chance to prove how tough he was. "I guess he didn't tell you why he wanted to kill me either."

"He said it was between you and him. I got the idea whatever it was happened some time ago."

That gave Redford nothing to go on. He could think of no reason why anyone would want to kill him. In the cavalry he'd had little time to make enemies, so it couldn't be anyone from there. And his Little Big Horn acquaintances were dead. Richie Hickley had reason enough to kill him because

Redford shot his brothers, but Richie also was dead. Redford had plenty to ponder.

"Are you gonna keep hanging around here?" Eden asked, eager to change the subject.

"I don't know yet. When I left for the army, Whitton said my deputy's badge would still be there if I wanted it when I got back. He said it again today."

Redford gave his head a bewildered shake, like there was something more he needed to get said. Stuff was piling up on him, for which he felt some responsibility. Who was the stranger Eden said was in a sweat to kill him? He couldn't even guess.

One thing was sure–he needed to get to San Saba and reconnect with Ashley, but something kept getting in the way. There was his commitment to Cal to look after Cassie, but she said nothing that sounded like she wanted to be looked after.

"There's something else I've got to take care of," Redford said, "before I can look too far down the road."

"What's that?" Eden said.

"I promised to look after Cassie if anything happened to Cal up there."

"You promised?"

"What do you say when a friend asks you in the middle of flying arrows and rifle shots to look after his wife if he gets killed? Cal asked me to, and I said I would."

"What does that include?" Eden asked.

"Whatever it takes, I guess."

"Does Cassie know that?"

"Not yet."

"Are you going to tell her?"

"She'll have to know. I can't just do nothing about it. But I'm not very high on her list of favorites right now. It's like I committed a crime because Cal died and I didn't."

Eden gave her head a solemn nod. "Why didn't you die?"

"Cassie asked me that too."

"Well, it's an obvious question. You told me two hundred and sixty eight men died at Little Big Horn, and you rode away from it. Anybody who knows that would wonder."

"I don't have an answer for that. All I know is, like I told you, when it was over the first thing I saw was Custer's body on top of me.

"I didn't know who it was till the fighting was over. The Sioux didn't know who they shot."

"Maybe they did," Eden said. Didn't you tell me you were on good terms with that Indian chief?"

Redford gave his shoulders a slight shrug, as though having had a pow-wow with Sitting Bull was a part of his job and didn't amount to much.

"Maybe they didn't kill you because you were friends with the chief," Eden said.

He passed her a look that told her he didn't think about it that way.

"Listen!" she said suddenly.

Redford cocked an ear toward the barroom downstairs.

"You hear that?" she asked.

He strode to the door and stuck his head out.

"I'm calling you out, black man!" came the voice of an angry young man from the barroom below.

"That's Cecil Covington," Eden said.

She scrambled out of bed, and swept up a robe to cover her body.

"I've got to go down there," she said.

Redford put out a hand.

"Wait," he said, and she stopped.

He went to the top of the stairs and looked out over the barroom.

Eden followed a step behind.

Play at the poker tables stopped. The players tossed in their hands and ran for cover. Wary punchers, smelling the makings of a gunfight, scrambled to safety. Some scampered out the door to avoid being hit by flying lead. Others lined up against the wall, eyes focused on Thomas Belt, sitting calmly at the table in the corner. Belt motioned to the burly Jake behind the bar for a coffee refill, and he brought the pot.

Cecil was facing Belt from twenty feet away, his feet spread apart in a challenging stance, his right hand hovering near his gun.

"Come on!" Cecil screamed. "Make your move."

Belt placed his coffee cup on the table, casually wiped the drippings from his chin. He held up both hands to let Cecil know he wasn't holding a weapon.

"Why don't you come over here and have a seat?" Belt said to Cecil. He pulled out a chair for the boy to sit on. "I'll ask that nice man over there to bring us another cup and some fresh coffee," Belt said, "and we can talk this thing over."

"No time for talk," Cecil shot back. "My pa says I better not show up out there again till I settle with you."

"And how do you plan to do that?"

"I–I–guess I gotta call you out."

"I don't want to kill you," Belt said.

Across his mind flashed the face of the only man he ever killed–that time in Mississippi. Bozo Cliff. The one he served time for.

Belt hoped a dose of common sense would sidetrack this youngster from making a tragic mistake–either killing or being killed. He also believed Cecil was not eager for a fight, but challenged him because his father goaded him into it.

"I got to do it, or my pa will skin my ass," Cecil said.

"Well, which would you rather have," Thomas said, "a skinned ass or a dead ass? If you call me out I'll have to kill you, and I don't think your pa would like that."

Cecil took a look at the punchers lined up around the wall. He could feel their eyes boring into his sweat-beaded face, waiting for him to make up his mind whether being dead from a black man's bullet would be worse than being skinned by his pa.

I've come this far, Cecil told himself. If he didn't finish the job the whole town would poke fun at him, and make him out to be a coward.

Cecil could almost feel the welts of his father's belt buckle on his backside if Jonas found out he backed down. He didn't like the odds, nor was he sure of his chances against the big black man. He lost to him before, and the time for stalling was over. He had to make some kind of move.

It took less than a minute for him to decide he wasn't ready to die. His gun hand hung loose. He slumped into the chair, facing Belt.

Belt waved at Jake. The slick-haired, sleeve-gartered bartender brought Cecil a cup and poured it full of coffee. "What's your name?"

"Cecil Covington."

"Son of Jonas Covington."

"How'd you know that?"

"How I know is not important," Belt said. "What is important is you're too young to die." He lowered his voice to a whisper. "Listen closely to what I'm about to say. When I lean back in this chair and wink at you, I want you to bounce up, whip out your gun, and wave it at me like you're gonna use it on me. I'll jump up with both hands in the air, and make a beeline for the front door. You fire a shot over my head, and I'll disappear out the door. That way you can go out there and tell your pa you ran Thomas Belt out of town. Can you do that?"

"I–I don't know, I–"

"It won't hurt half as bad as a skinned ass."

"Well, I–"

Belt leaned back in his chair, winked at Cecil, and Cecil went for his gun. From the stair landing, Redford saw Belt take off and make it out the batwings just ahead of Cecil's wild shot.

Cecil took a long look at the door to be sure Belt was gone. He checked the wide-eyed spectators who had trouble believing what they saw. Was Cecil Covington running the black man out of town? With a gun in his hand firing one wild shot? Cecil holstered his gun, and headed for the door.

The bodies against the wall relaxed, and Eden Fletcher went to get some clothes on.

Redford came down the stairway to talk to Jake. "What started the ruckus?"

"Danged if I know." Jake wiped his hands on his soiled white apron, and shoved the black sleeve garters up past his elbows. "The boy said he was calling the black man out. Things settled down to a turtle crawl. All of a sudden, the Covington boy pulled a gun on him, and the Negro high-tailed it out like a scared rabbit, and Cecil slung a shot at him."

Uh-huh, Redford mused. Like a scared rabbit? Not likely.

Sheriff Whitton burst through the door. "What the hell is going on here?" he demanded of no one in particular. Nobody answered. "Who was that black man I just saw taking off on that white horse?"

Redford answered, "Thomas Belt."

Whitton's face turned white. "Who? Belt you say?"

"Thomas Belt," Redford said again.

The sheriff took off out the back way, asking no more questions to which he didn't want to hear the answers.

Play at the poker tables resumed. Curious punchers muttering among themselves, elbowed up to the bar, wondering what the fracas was all about.

Redford doubted Cecil's threat was responsible for Belt's sudden departure. He heard Thomas' voice.

"If I leave it won't be because they scared me

off."

Redford filed the incident in the back of his mind and split the batwings, on his way out. He swung into the saddle, heard a shot. A bullet whizzed past his head, and plunged into the Bang Tail's door post. Redford slid out of the saddle, and drew his gun. He ran a zig-zag pattern into the front door of Oscar Doke's hardware store.

"Redford?" Doke squeaked, decked out in nightcap and floor length cotton gown'.

"It's me," Redford answered.

"What's going on?" With a trembling hand, Oscar raked his pale forehead.

"Somebody took a shot at me. I thought maybe it came from here."

"I heard the shot," Oscar said, "but nobody fired from here."

Redford holstered his gun and left Oscar shaking in his white stockinged feet.

"Redford!"

Redford heard the voice, and checked the darkness for a face that went with it. He saw none. Half way to where his horse was tied, he heard it again.

"Redford!"

Redford wheeled around and faced a young man stepping into the lamplight of Doke's front window. A shock of black hair brushed his shoulders, and a Colt .44 nudged his right thigh.

It was Emitt Coldwater.

Redford didn't know that. Till now, he didn't care who the man was, where he came from, nor why he was there. Unless he was the one who told

Eden he was going to kill him. That would rustle up some concern. Redford was thirty-six years old and pegged the young man at hardly more than half that.

"You *are* Redford, ain't you?" Coldwater said.

"Who's asking?"

"I aim to kill you, Redford."

Killers came in all shapes and sizes, but none of them Redford ever saw flashed an "I'm gonna kill you" sign on their foreheads. Even so, he figured the best way to deal with this one, who was dumb enough to tell him he was going to kill him, was to keep a cool head, with a ready gun hand in case he made a move to back up his threat.

This must be the one Eden told me about, Redford mused. "Why do you want to kill me?"

"It ain't want to. It's going to."

"There must be some reason why you think I need to be dead."

"There's a reason."

"Get it done then."

"In good time." Why was he stalling, Coldwater argued with himself, but caution stilled his hand. "I'm giving you time to think about it," he said.

"I've already thought about it," Redford said.

"When the time comes, you'll know why." Redford was not the man he had expected to face. *If you're gonna do it, get it done! That's what you came for. You rode all those miles to do it, so–*

"You better do it now," Redford said with a foot in the stirrup. "There may not be another time." He threw a leg over the saddle, showing Coldwater his back.

"When I'm ready, Redford," Coldwater said.

"You're a damn fool for telling me," Redford tossed over his shoulder.

Coldwater slipped back into the night.

Redford reined the bay toward the west edge of town on his way to see Cassie. Still, he couldn't help wondering why that man seemed determined to kill him. He couldn't be too anxious, or he'd have done it–or tried–when he had the chance.

Redford had enough to deal with at the moment. It was time he got things straight with Cassie. He couldn't dismiss the matter of Thomas Belt who rode all the way from God only knew where in search of his father.

That had nothing to do with Cassie. She didn't know who Thomas Belt was, nor whether Thomas could have killed Cecil Covington if it came to a showdown. And the threat of the brash young stranger, Cassie couldn't care less about. Nor would she care that a half hour ago he crawled out of bed with Eden Fletcher. None of those things would bring more than a blank look of disinterest from Cassie Courtney.

He did some strong thinking about what he was supposed to do to keep his promise to Cal. He still wasn't sure, but it must be settled with his widow. She likely would slough off anything he said, but it had to be said.

Wondering what kind of reception he'd get this time, he dropped a rein over the white picket gate post, strode to Cassie's front door, and gave it a couple of knuckle raps. A thin spiral of gray smoke curled up out of the chimney against the moonlit night, and a coal oil lamp flickered in the front room window.

As he approached Cassie's house he caught a glimpse of her peeking out from behind a window curtain, but she didn't answer his knock. Looking back on their earlier meeting, he wouldn't be surprised if she greeted him this time of night with a shotgun aimed at his nose.

"Cassie," he called. Still no answer.

He knocked again and waited.

A moment later the door flew open, and in it stood the once attractive young woman, haggard and red-eyed, with puffy cheeks, hair mussed up. No shotgun did she point at his nose.

"Hello, Cassie."

"What the hell are you doing here?" she asked, drawing her robe close around her waist.

"I know it's late, but we need to talk."

"I don't want to hear anything you've got to say."

"Maybe you do. Can I come in?"

She glared at him for a long moment before she threw up her hands, flung the door open, and stormed away in a huff.

Redford stepped inside.

"I've got nothing to say to you," she said.

"All right. But, I've got something to say to you."

Stalking away, she did an abrupt about-face with fire in her eyes.

"So, talk," she said.

"Cal Courtney was the best young soldier I ever knew," Redford said. "He trained hard, he fought hard, and he was afraid of nothing. It wasn't my fault he was killed, and if I could have saved him, he'd be here instead of me. At a time like that, an arrow or rifle shot can come from any direction. One of them hit Cal."

"He died up there because of a power crazy man whose only thought was of making a name for himself."

Dan trained his gaze on her anger-red face.

"Cal's only thought was of you," he went on. "He loved the army, but he loved you more than anything else.

"He didn't join up only because he wanted to, but because he had to. Men like Cal can't rest until they whip whatever it is that's pushing them.

"His push was to be a soldier, get it out of his system, then come back to you.

"The last word I heard him say was your name."

Redford didn't share with her Cal's confession that he wanted to "do something" to make Cassie proud of him.

"Cal asked me to look after you if anything–" He waved a hand, letting the thought complete itself. "I told him I would."

She stiffened straight as a poker. "I don't need you to look after me!" she said, eyes flashing, mouth hard and set. "The coward of Little Big Horn! What could I possibly need that you could do for me?"

She strode to the door, threw it open, and stood aside, a fiery invitation for him to leave. "There's nothing you can do," she said, "except bring back my husband."

Stunned, Redford stared into her unforgiving

eyes. He hesitated for a silent moment. She had a right to be upset, but he didn't kill Cal, and took no responsibility for his death. Yes, he had encouraged Cal to join the Cavalry because it was the best place for him. It offered a better chance of returning home to his young bride. But there was nothing to be gained by debating the matter with her. Her mind was made up. With a silent nod, he turned away.

She slammed the door shut behind him. Leaning with her back to the door, she buried her face in her hands–and wept.

CHAPTER 11

Why Harvey went west

When the last gunshot marked the end of the War Between the States, life for freed slaves in the South offered little more than before the war. Six hundred thousand young men, Blue and Gray, lost their lives "to preserve the Union" for President Lincoln. White planters owned all the land, refusing to sell the freedmen ground fertile enough to grow crops.

Harvey Belt tried without success to raise corn, beans, and potatoes in the red Mississippi dirt the planters didn't want. One sweltering afternoon, Harvey paused for breath in the middle of what he was trying to chop and dig into a potato patch. He rested his pick handle against a knee, and raked a shirt sleeve across his sweat-soaked brow.

He heard someone call his name. He jerked his

head around and watched the leisurely approach of his friend Abner. The grinning Abner, a former slave himself, dug into his pocket and brought out a sheet of yellow paper with printing on it. He poked it at Harvey. It was a flier encouraging freedmen to migrate to an all-black community called Nicodemus, settled in western Kansas by a group of freedmen.

On the plantations, it was against the law for slaves to learn to read. Even so, Master Minwell's wife insisted that "even slaves deserved the right to read and do numbers." Harvey didn't attend the secret classes in her fruit cellar, but he made sure his son Thomas did.

Harvey looked at the flier from Abner, but pleaded "bad eyesight."

"That's all right," Abner said. "My boy told me what it say–forty acres and a mule. The gov'ment gonna give 'em to you."

Harvey scoffed at that.

He didn't know anything about Kansas, and never heard of Nicodemus, except for the man the Lord dealt with in the Bible he heard preachers going on about. Anyhow, if the government had anything to do with whatever Abner was asking him to believe, it couldn't amount to much.

"Gov'ment don't give nobody nothin'," Harvey protested. "Mr. Lincoln's paper say we don't have to slave no more. Well, we still slavin'."

"I hear ye," Abner said.

"All the gov'ment does is take away what Mister Lincoln give us. We just a bunch o' black folks that ain't got nothin', never had nothin', and never will have nothin'."

Abner insisted. "All you gotta do is work the ground for five years and it belong to you."

"Yeah?" said the skeptic. "How come you ain't gone?"

"Who? Me?" his grinning friend said. "Too stove up to make the trip plum out there."

Harvey grunted, told Abner goodbye, and went back to work.

Lying in bed that night, Harvey gave Abner's flier a good thinking. He decided he'd do as well in Kansas as in the middle of a Mississippi red dirt patch that wouldn't grow beans.

With a shake of his frowzy gray head, Harvey was sad Thomas was still locked up for killing Bozo Cliff. He didn't want to go as far away as Kansas on the chance that somehow Thomas might be coming home. After talking it over with his wife Alisha, however, they knew Thomas's release was unlikely. Whatever the future held, they must plan for the two of them.

So, hoping it would work out for the good, they agreed. Harvey would go ahead to Nicodemus. If there was a reason to stay there, he'd send word for Alisha to join one of the groups making the trek from Mississippi to Kansas.

It took Harvey three days, and more holes in his already thin shoe soles, to walk to Vicksburg. Once there, he plunked down eight crumpled greenbacks for a boat ride up the Mississippi to St. Louis. He joined a group of impatient, frustrated freedmen aboard a steamer whose departure from Vicksburg was delayed. He stewed for days, afraid the boat would never set sail.

It did.

When the boat's whistle finally blared, and the hawsers were lifted, he was caught up in a wave of joyful shouts. "We headin' for the promise land!" burst from the throats of the former slaves on their way to Nicodemus.

At St. Louis they were herded onto another boat, docked on the Missouri River, that sailed west across Missouri to Wyandotte, Kansas. Their destination was Nicodemus, where no white folks would tell them what they could or could not do. They'd be free to choose their own way, and enjoy the rights and privileges denied them on the plantations.

At Wyandotte, he joined a group of immigrants from Kentucky, headed west on foot, bound for the New Eden at Nicodemus.

When he arrived in Kansas, Harvey was disappointed in what Nicodemus offered, and his hope for a better life was shattered. No churches were found, no schools, and none of the places of business touted by the fliers. Nor did Harvey find the fertile ground the promoters promised as bait to lure former slaves from the Southland to the "promised land" of western Kansas.

The dry, hard prairie sod didn't grow much of anything, except buffalo grass, good for the buffalo, not good enough to grow potatoes and corn any better than had the red dirt he left behind in Mississippi. And the ear-shattering honk of the expected mule for pulling a plow he never heard.

The pick axe could hardly pierce the surface of

the parched earth, trampled for generations by the hooves of rumbling buffalo.

Even so, some ex-slaves came and stayed, working the ground with bent backs and calloused hands from daylight till dark.

"We prob'ly as good off here as any other place," they rationalized.

But for Harvey Belt it was not good enough, holding little promise for his family's future.

It was time to move on. Harvey left Nicodemus behind, and struck out on his own across a strange country. He wasn't sure where his weary legs might take him in search of some place where he could make a living, and start a new life. He sent word to Mississippi, telling Alisha not to come "till I get hooked up some place better."

Setting a steady course north, he didn't know his search for "some place better" would end at a place called Whiskey Flats. In Oscar Doke's hardware store he met a man from the Bar T Ranch. The man told Harvey his smithy took off and didn't come back. He asked Harvey if he could blacksmith.

On the plantation, Harvey learned to stoke the red hot coals, and pound a piece of raw metal into a plow share, chopping hoe, or digging shovel. He told the man he could, and the next day he went to work as a blacksmith on the Bar T Ranch.

In the Bang Tail Saloon one Saturday night, Harvey got into a disagreement with a couple of cowhands from another outfit who crabbed about "drinkin' with some damn nigger crowdin' my elbow."

Harvey was a free man. He took issue with their

remarks, and the two of them took him on. Harvey whipped them both, and sent them slinking away nursing their wounds.

Sheriff Demp Whitton showed up, took a brief look around, and arrested Harvey for disturbing the peace. Harvey insisted he didn't start the trouble, and the two who did were the ones who should be going to jail. He protested louder, and a roughneck named Rance Gomer looped a rope around Harvey's neck and dragged him behind his horse to the edge of town.

Cheered on by a handful of whiskey-soaked cronies, Gomer threw the loose end of the rope over an oak limb, tied it to his saddle horn, and pulled it taut. Harvey's feet cleared the ground. Gasping for breath, he was already half dead from being dragged by the neck.

Now he was. Gomer and his loop-legged friends laughed with hyena shrieks, and riddled Harvey's dangling body with gunshots.

In the annals of Kansas, historians will find no record of the lynching of Harvey Belt.

Even so, old timers will tell you it happened in Whiskey Flats, Kansas, April 27, 1876.

Unaware of Harvey's lynching, Thomas's mother Alisha was lying on her Mississippi deathbed. Longing for her son who was serving his time in that white man's Mississippi prison, she clung to the hope that any day now, her husband would be coming home, or, at least, Harvey would arrange for her to join him in Kansas.

As a slave on Felix Minwell's plantation, Alisha contracted a debilitating disease for which Minwell provided no medical attention.

"Why should I waste good money on some old woman who can't pick or hoe anymore?" he sneered.

Alisha's condition grew worse.

General Lee's surrender at Appomattox Court House gave her the freedom to seek help for herself, but she never saw the inside of a doctor's office, and declared, "I sure ain't goin' in now!"

Alisha had no idea where Nicodemus was, except what Harvey told her about Abner's flier. If Harvey was still there, she wanted to be there too. Aside from the expectation of one day leaving for the West, there was little for Alisha to live for, except for her son Thomas stuck away in that prison.

She didn't know whether she would see him again, but pride in her son knew no bounds, having told him to "go to school so you can amount to somethin'."

Not since they locked him up "for what he done to that evil man," had she seen Thomas. Every day she thanked God for Judge Malcom Conover, dispatched from New Jersey to the South after the war to preside over such cases. The judge reduced Thomas's sentence from "death by hanging" to life in prison.

Thomas was twelve years old when he learned to hate the field boss, Bozo Cliff. Cliff lashed his father with a bone-tipped thong, the day his father was sick with a fever. Harvey recalled the cruel punishment of others who had feigned illness to escape a day's work. He dared not tell the boss he was not able to make it to the field. Half way along the cotton row, Harvey collapsed into his basket. He stumbled to his feet, gathered a few more handfuls of cotton, dropped them into the basket, and crumpled to the ground in a heap.

"You lazy lout!" Cliff screamed at Harvey.

Flailing away with his whip on the back of the fallen slave, Cliff kept shouting at Harvey to "get up and get back to work!"

Finally, Harvey was able to lift himself to his hands and knees. Wracked with pain, he struggled to his feet, and went back to work. By day's end Harvey was hardly able to drag himself to the cabin door. With loving hands and tearful eyes, Alisha bathed his wounds and put him to bed.

Before the sun got up the next morning, Harvey rolled his stiff, aching body out of bed. Alisha served him grits, hog fat, and black coffee. Against his wife's pleas, Harvey forced his body out the door, and joined the other field hands on their way to work.

At times Harvey thought he'd be better off dead, but he strove to stay alive, enduring the harsh treatment of the man with the whip.

Etched on the mind of Thomas Belt, he saw yet the welts, the lacerations, the blood, and the suffering of his beaten father. Through his body flowed sorrow for him, well aware that life beyond the borders of the plantation was an impossible dream.

Black people lived with degradation and humiliation from one generation to the next, and talking about anything better was a waste of time.

Thomas promised himself that someday–some day!–he would make Bozo Cliff pay for what he did to his father.

And he did.

Thomas was twenty-two years old when the war ended. Jubilant shouts of "I'm free! I'm free!" echoed across the Southland. Watching the pandemonium around him, just thinking about it filled Thomas's mind with wonder. His whole life he lived in slavery. What did it mean to be free?

Crowding his mind was the promise he made himself to avenge his father's punishment. It took a while for Thomas to understand he could go anywhere he wanted, and do whatever he wanted without asking anybody if it was all right. No "boss man" threatened with a whip, no "Massa" to bow down to when he passed by.

Did freedom include paying back the man who beat his sick father? He didn't mean to kill Bozo Cliff, but he wanted to hurt him.

In his search for work, Thomas one day came upon a road gang. One of the men Thomas recognized was Bozo Cliff, overseeing the crew with a shovel in his hand. Thomas approached Cliff, reminding him of who he was–the son of Harvey Belt.

"Belt?" Cliff sneered. "That don't mean nothin' to me."

"It does to me," Thomas said. "He's my father. You nearly beat him to death one day when he was so sick he couldn't stand up."

"Yeah? Well, hell! You expect me to remember stuff like that? That was a long time ago."

"Not long enough," Thomas said. "I made up my mind I'd make you pay for that."

With a derisive grin, Cliff said, "Well, now ain't that somethin'? And how do you figger on gettin' that done, boy?"

"Drop that shovel and I'll show you."

Cliff didn't drop the shovel. He swung it at Thomas. Thomas knocked the shovel out of Cliff's hands, and bull-butted him with a headlong dive. They rolled around in the muddy red dirt, trading punches, most of which didn't land.

Cliff scrambled to his feet and worked his way toward the shovel. He grabbed it up and swung it again, but Thomas dodged away. He grabbed the shovel, ripped it out of Cliff's hands, and swung it at him. The solid blow to the head put the former field boss on the ground.

A friend of Cliff's knelt beside him where the field boss lay motionless. "He's dead, man," the friend said to Thomas.

Thomas was hauled away in shackles, found guilty in a white man's court of killing the former slave driver, and began his term in prison. In his seventh year behind bars, an earth tremor shattered the prison's ancient stone walls, and left the cell doors in shambles.

Eluding the law, the ruthless slave hunters, night riders, and the spine chilling threat of baying bloodhounds, Thomas headed for home. He raced through fields of cotton, indigo, and tobacco. He splashed across streams, lungs near to bursting. He dared not stop to rest, but forced his weary body to keep going, thinking only of reaching his mother before she drew her dying breath. As though willing herself not to die before she saw her son one more time, his mother was still alive. Thomas stole through the house to the back bedroom.

Spooning hot chicken broth into her mouth when she grew too weak to feed herself, Thomas did what he could to make his mother comfortable.

The pain grew so severe she pleaded with God to take her. The day she turned sixty-three, He did.

With her dying gasp, Alisha's bony fingers squeezed Thomas's hand for the last time. "Find your daddy," she wheezed.

And so it was, on a blistering day in July, 1876, Thomas Belt rode a white horse down the middle of Parker Street in Whiskey Flats, Kansas, and sampled the coffee at Eden Fletcher's Bang Tail Saloon.

He would learn that his father's body dangled at the end of a lynch mob's rope.

* * * *

Redford to the rescue

An eight-year-old boy in striped overalls and a frazzled straw hat burst into the Bang Tail Saloon and screamed, "Cassie's house is on fire!"

When Preacher Haskell pulled the bell rope in the church's steeple it usually was to remind the citizens of Whiskey Flats that it was time to head for Sunday morning preaching. Any other time it was to sound the alarm that something unusual, sometimes tragic, was taking place.

Now, on a Saturday night, the toll of the bell brought the townspeople pouring out of shops, stores, and saloons, swarming to where the flames from Cassie's burning house lit up the sky.

Redford didn't wait to ask questions. He leaped onto the bay and took off at a dead run.

The horse-drawn water wagon careened around the corner with dogs nipping at the heels of the frenzied steeds.

Redford outran the fire wagon to Cassie's, where hungry fingers of fire lapped at the roof of the wood frame house. He rolled off the bay and made a beeline for Cassie's front door, shouldered it open, and started feeling his way through the smoke and flames.

"Cassie!" he yelled, throwing up his arms to protect his face from the heat. "Cassie, it's Redford! Where are you? Cassie!"

He heard a choking cough to his right and reached out a hand, and eased his way through the smoke toward where the cough came from. He flattened out on the floor, and covered his mouth and nose with one hand. With the other he felt his way below the roiling smoke.

She coughed again.

"Cassie!" His hand struck something soft. "Cassie!"

"Leave me alone," she cried from where she collapsed on the bedroom floor. "I don't want to live anymore!"

He gathered her in his arms and stumbled toward the door. Cassie fought to free herself, but Redford held her close, protecting her from the flames.

Blinded by clouds of smoke and fire, he could only guess he was headed in the right direction.

Finally, he made his way to the front door, a staggered out into the yard then placed Cassie on the ground. Her face was red from the heat, her skirt scorched and still smoldering around the hem. Redford ripped the skirt off, and someone spread a coat over her. "You're going to be all right," Redford said to the sobbing girl.

"Let me die," she moaned. "I want to be with Cal!"

"Cal wouldn't want that," he said. "I told you he asked me to look after you."

"The best thing you can do for me is to leave me alone!"

"I'll take care of her." It was Eden at his elbow. She knew how terrifying it was to fight her way out of a fire ravaged house. "She can stay with me."

Redford carried the sobbing girl to the Bang Tail Saloon, and placed her in one of Eden's upstairs rooms. He fought the notion that Cassie intentionally set her house on fire.

CHAPTER 12

Thomas meets the preacher

The Reverend George Haskell looked up from his desk in the office of his Whiskey Flats Baptist Church. "Oh," said he. In his doorway stood a husky black man staring at him, waiting to be invited in.

"I'm sorry if I disturbed you, sir," said Thomas Belt. "I guess you didn't hear me come in."

"I'm the one who should apologize," Haskell said. "I sometimes get so caught up in preparing my Sunday sermon everything else floats right over my head."

He stood up and put out his hand. Belt clasped it in a strong handshake. "I'm George Haskell. I work here."

"Thomas Belt."

"Yes, I heard about you. Your name came up at breakfast at Mrs. O'Rourke's. It has been a while since we had a Negro in our community."

"Do you remember the last one?"

"Yes, I do. I never knew him, but I heard his name. It was Belt, and he–" Haskell cast Thomas a questioning look.

"Harvey Belt?" Thomas said.

Haskell put a thoughtful palm to his chin. "I believe that's right, and you're– Are you a relative of his?"

"He's my father. He used to go to church with my mother, and I was hoping you could tell me something about where I might look for him. We haven't heard from him for quite some time. My mother died a while back. She wanted me to find my father."

"Mr. Belt, I must confess I don't know much about your father."

Haskell was aware that Harvey was hanged by a drunken mob, but he thought it best to leave the details to someone who was there, someone who could more accurately describe what took place.

"I don't recall that your father attended my services, but I can put you in touch with a man who knows more about him than I do."

The preacher cupped Thomas's elbow in his right hand, and steered him toward the door. "The man I speak of lives out south of town a way," he said. "His name is Baker Wainwright. Baker won't be hard to find."

George closed the door behind the departing Thomas Belt, and gave his head a sorrowful shake.

Belt mounted his white horse and gigged him into a comfortable gait heading south. He looked forward to meeting Baker Wainwright, hoping Wainwright could shed some light on the whereabouts of his father.

CHAPTER 13

Whitton's unhappy ride

Demp cringed at the thought of another stream of vindictive words from Jonas's vitriolic tongue. Why had he put up with it for so long? The answer was simple but bitter: Thirty dollars a month.

Whitton rode out to tell Jonas what he knew about the Negro man who showed up in town–with the same name as the black man lynched by a handful of drunken wranglers. One of whom was Jonas's son Jubal.

Demp nudged his horse through the gate arched by the white oak sign with "Covington" burnt into it. In no hurry to get there, he slowed his gray mount to a walk toward the rambling stone house overlooking the valley to the trout stream below. Demp's eyes swept the long, low stables, the-two-pole corrals, the sandstone outbuildings, and the wranglers' bunk house beyond. Things he'd seen many times but hardly noticed till now. For some reason he couldn't explain, Demp was struck by something deep inside telling him this might be his last ride to the Circle C.

Demp owed Jonas. For the past twelve years Jonas paid his salary. Though he was not anxious for this encounter with the tempestuous rancher, it had to be done.

He dismounted, climbed the six stone steps to the front door, and gave it a fisted rap.

From inside the house, a gruff voice roared, "Come in!"

Demp took a deep breath, and eased open the heavy wooden door. He made his way through the front room to the back of the house and the office where he knew he would find Jonas Covington. The rancher was mulling over a stack of papers spread on the big desk his father carved out of an oak stump when Jonas was nine years old.

This was not the first time Whitton faced the rancher with misgiving. Covington was the well from which sprang the means by which Demp fed and clothed his wife and kids. He sometimes came to pay respects to the source of his livelihood. This time was different. While he was grateful for Jonas's generosity, Demp admitted to himself for the first time–no amount of money could buy his respect for the tempestuous rancher. And this, indeed, may be the last time he would stand, hat in hand, humiliated by Jonas Covington.

In his early years, Whitton was respected as a

tough, by-the-book lawman, though he never compared himself to the famous lawmen portrayed in the dime novels. Still, in his younger days, Whitton was quick with a gun. He killed in his job as lawman, but never thought of himself as a killer. He couldn't walk in the boots of the gunfighters, and he knew it.

Demp's best days were behind him, now playing out his time as sheriff of Whiskey Flats as the pawn of Jonas Covington. He mellowed in recent years, and served at the discretion of the biggest rancher in the county and only so long as Jonas continued to pay his wages.

Twelve years ago Jonas first picked up the tab for Demp's services, when the county ran out of money to pay a lawman. By the time the county coffers grew enough to cover Demp's pay, most people forgot they weren't already doing it, and Covington kept handing him thirty dollars every month.

Demp was a few years younger than Covington's sixty-four. He knew it was about time when most men with legal authority turned in their badges, folded up their gun belts, and stowed them away for the last time in bureau drawers. Demp confessed privately that he wondered what it would take for him to hang 'em up and call it good. Jonas's reaction to his son's involvement in the Harvey Belt hanging might well provide the answer for Demp.

He faced Jonas with a queasy stomach. He knew the rancher wouldn't want to hear what he came to say, but he dared not risk his hearing it from someone else. Jonas had to know Jubal took part in the hanging of Harvey Belt, and Whitton had to tell him. Whitton didn't want talk about what he, Sheriff Demp Whitton, could have done to stop the hanging, but made no move to do so.

He gave his hat a nervous twist between sweating palms. "Something has come up," he said to Jonas.

He was right. Covington didn't like the ominous tone he heard in the sheriff's voice.

"Like what?" Jonas said with a wrinkled brow.

"That black man who rode into town–"

"Yeah?" Jonas's mind flipped back to the one who shot Cecil. "Is that the first black man you ever saw?" he asked.

"No, sir, but this one's name is Belt," Demp answered.

"Belt?"

"Yes, sir. Thomas Belt."

Jonas cast him a questioning glance. Cecil told him he ran Belt out of town. If so, why was the sheriff so worked up about him?

He waited for Whitton to tell him.

"I don't know if he's kin to Harvey," Demp said, "but it don't look good."

"Harvey–?"

"Harvey Belt."

"Is he the one they strung up a while back?"

"Yes, sir."

"Who was in charge of that?"

Whitton hesitated. The only way to say it was to say it.

"One of your men put the noose around Harvey's neck," Whitton said.

"One of my men? Which one?"

"Gomer."

"Rance Gomer put the noose around Harvey Belt's neck?"

"Yes, sir."

"That saddle tramp son of a bitch!" Jonas raged. "I never should have taken him on. I figured bad blood was running through his veins the first time I saw him, but I needed help with the herd.

"I'll see that he gets taken care of!"

"I understand he's gone," Whitton said.

"Gone? Gomer's gone? Where the hell has he gone?" He wondered why he hadn't seen the wayward drifter hanging around lately.

"Somebody said he lit out after Belt threw him out of the Bang Tail."

Jonas engaged in a moment of silent rage. He knew about the incident between Belt and Gomer, but dismissed it when Cecil told him Belt left town.

"Did Belt know Gomer hung his father?" Jonas said.

"I don't think so."

"And you say there might be some connection between Harvey and this man you're talking about?"

"Well, I—"

"What's the matter with you, Whitton?" Covington roared, making no effort to disguise his anger. "A black man rides into town and you don't know where he came from, and you don't know if he's the son of a man they lynched. You're the law in this county, Whitton. It's your job to find out what the hell is going on when a stranger shows up.

For twelve years I've seen to it that you kept wearing that star. Maybe you're beginning to slow down some. Is that it?"

"No, sir, but–"

"Did this Belt fellow break the law?"

"Well, he's the one who shot Cecil."

There was Jonas's answer. "Belt is the one that shot my boy?" Not waiting for Whitton's response, he bellowed, "Then the black man is sure as hell the one who broke the law!"

"From what I've heard, Cecil egged him into it."

"I don't give a damn about who egged who into it. You're saying this Thomas Belt is

Harvey's son?"

"Like I said," Demp said, "I'm not sure yet."

"Well, when you get sure, there'll be time enough to do something about it," Jonas said. "Don't come whining to me till you've got something solid to talk about."

Whitton took deep breath. "There is one other thing."

"Yeah?" Jonas's ears were already full of more than he wanted to hear. "What's that?"

Demp didn't want to say it, but it had to be said. "One of the men in the hanging party was a son of yours."

Jonas's heavy black eyebrows came together in a point above his nose.

"Are you telling me one of my boys was mixed up in that hanging?"

"Yes, sir, he was," Whitton said, close to swallowing his Adam's apple.

"Which boy are you talking about?" Jonas was

sure he already knew the answer. "Cecil?"

"No, sir, it wasn't Cecil."

"Well, then who the hell was it?"

"Jubal."

Jonas stared at him for a furious minute. His eyes flashed, his face red with rage. Jubal? Jubal couldn't find his ass with both hands without help! How could anybody with as little mind as Jubal get involved in a hanging?

Jonas wiped his sweating forehead with an open palm, stroked his chin, searching for something to say that would counter what Whitton said about Jubal. He got up from his chair and paced a few steps back and forth behind the desk, trying to figure out what part his simple minded son played in such a vile act. When he was ready, Jonas looked at Whitton like Demp never saw before.

"Demp," Jonas said with unsettling calm, "what do you make of it?"

"I don't know, Jonas," Whitton said, relieved at being addressed with a civil tongue. "But if this Thomas Belt is Harvey's son, he'll be looking for somebody to pay for the hanging."

"Meaning my son?"

"Jubal was there."

"You say Jubal was there," Jonas said. "Does that mean you were there, too?"

Whitton gave his head a sorrowful shake.

"Did you try to stop it?" Jonas said.

"Things got out of hand," Demp said, humbling himself in the presence of the mighty.

"Why in hell didn't you try to stop it?"

"I just–it was–"

"You didn't do anything about it," Jonas said, on the edge of rage, "and now you're telling me my boy was in on the hanging! You're the sheriff of this county, Whitton. What the hell do you think I pay you for?"

"Mr. Covington, I–"

"How come you never told me about this before?"

"I don't know. I guess I thought– You know, a black man– A bunch of likkered up punchers–"

"Did you see Jubal there?"

"Yes, sir, I saw him."

"What was he doing there?"

Demp had trouble getting it out. "He grabbed Harvey and threw him against the wall."

"Is that against the law?"

"Well, no but–"

"If Jubal didn't break the law, what kind of trouble can he be in?"

"I just thought, if this Thomas Belt comes looking for people who took part in the hanging, you ought to know Jubal was one of them."

"You damn right I ought to know! You waited a hell of a long time to tell me about it. Belt shot one of my boys, and now you're saying another one was involved in hanging his old man."

Jonas raked a hand across his face, as though something else just came to mind. "What about Redford?" Jonas asked. "Somebody said he was back in town. I hear he's the only man who walked away from that Little Big Horn outfit."

"I don't know about that, but he's back."

"Is he wearing that star again?"

"Not yet. We haven't talked about it."

"Is he in cahoots with the black man?"

"Not that I know of."

"All right. You go on back to town. I'll talk to my boys and decide what to do about this."

"Yes, sir."

"And, Demp," Jonas said.

"Sir?"

"See if you can find something to do that makes it look like you're in charge. Do you think you can do that?"

"Yes, sir."

Demp plopped his hat on, slunk out of the house, crawled dejectedly into the saddle, and reined toward town.

Who the hell did Jonas Covington think he's messing with?

CHAPTER 14

Who killed my father?

Thomas Belt reined his white stallion to a halt near the front door of the thatch roofed house a mile south of town. To his nose came the tantalizing aroma of gray smoke rising from a wood-burning fireplace, swirling lazily above the stone chimney. Blue morning glories and red geraniums flourished in the flower beds around the front door of the log house.

Sight of the house took Thomas back to the slave cabin where he was born, where his parents lived on Felix Minwell's plantation before the Civil War. They spent their lives in the small cabin with its dirt floor, hardly big enough for two straw pallets and a wood-burning fireplace–the only home they knew.

From the slave quarters they could see the great

house of the wealthy landowner rising to its imposing three-story height. His parents never saw the mansion's hand-carved walnut furniture and winding mahogany staircase, so they didn't know what to dream for. They did dream that somewhere beyond the borders of the oppressive plantation were places of greater comfort than their rough-hewn log cabin.

Thomas recalled the painful years his father and mother labored from daylight till dark hoeing weeds, thinning cotton rows, and filling straw baskets with the fluffy white stuff. Nights of tossing and turning, seeking rest from the aches and pains of back breaking work.

He recalled with misty eyes the times his father, so tired he couldn't take another step, crawled the last fifty feet to the cabin door on his hands and knees. He heard again the tearful pleas of his mother to a merciful God to protect his father from being traded to that planter in a distant part of Mississippi.

She knew if they took Harvey away, she would never see him again. As though receiving an answer to her prayers, the following day Alisha shouted and wept joyful tears at the news sweeping like wildfire across the Southland: General Robert E. Lee surrendered to Ulysses S. Grant at Appomattox Court House! The war was over!

Thomas lived again the boundless joy in his mother's eyes. The end of the fighting meant his father would not be hauled away. Harvey suddenly became what Mister Lincoln called "a free man." He could go anyplace he wanted, no longer the chattel of the white master. Even so, Harvey soon learned that freedmen were still looked down upon as slaves, with no souls, and no rights.

The sound of a creaking door brought Thomas back to the house on the banks of the stream to where George Haskell directed him. In the doorway appeared an elderly man with a shotgun cradled in the crook of his left arm. "Hello, out there," the man called from the doorway, half hidden by gathering shadows. "Who's there?"

"Thomas Belt. Are you Mr. Wainwright?"

"I'm Baker Wainwright. What is it you want?"

"I'm looking for my father. George Haskell in town said you might be able to help me."

"Haskell? The preacher?"

"Yes, sir."

"Well, get down off that horse," Wainwright said, lowering the shotgun, "and come in this house."

Wainwright supported Haskell's initial efforts to build the church in Whiskey Flats. Born and raised in the southern tradition of middle Tennessee, Wainwright grew up in the Cumberland Presbyterian Church. He didn't subscribe to everything the Baptist minister preached in Whiskey Flats, but what he heard from Haskell's pulpit was better than the nothing the town heard before.

Wainwright believed a church would contribute to the growth of the community, and made a financial contribution to help get it built. When it was completed, he continued with offerings to help keep it alive. Wainwright respected George as the first person with the courage to build a church in the rough and tumble town of Whiskey Flats, Kansas.

Belt dismounted and followed the limping older man inside. Wainwright was slight of build with graying hair and a twinkle in his aging eyes.

"Bethy," he said to the woman he introduced as his wife. "Bring this man a cup of coffee."

Bethy was a plump, cherry-cheeked woman of sixty-three. Her gray streaked brown hair was knotted into a bun at the back of her head. Her face glowed with a pleasant smile. She and Baker recently celebrated forty-seven years of married life. They reared four sons, all of whom opposed their father's view on slavery, perceiving it as a crime against humanity.

Baker and Bethy encouraged the sons to choose sides according to their sympathies, aside from the political aspects of the war. The boys chose to fight on the side of the Union, and hadn't been heard from since. Though they received no official notice, the parents were resigned to the probability that the boys did not survive the war.

Still, Bethy harbored hope that one day her sons would come roaring back, and show up at their door with happy smiles, hungry as wolves, as before they rode away to fight a war. Baker shared her hope for their sons' return. He informed friends and relatives in Tennessee of their whereabouts, in the event the boys should return. The war ended eleven years ago, and time chipped away at the likelihood that the Wainwright boys would be coming home.

While sympathizing with the Southerners' right to make rules for themselves, including the right to hold slaves, the Wainwrights held none when they lived in Tennessee. Indeed, in support of the states' rights, Baker served on the staff of General Lee. Two days before Lee's surrender, Wainwright lost his left leg below the knee in a skirmish outside Richmond. A wooden peg was strapped to the knee, accounting for the limp Thomas noticed when he followed the older man into the house.

Studying the face of his guest, Baker sensed he was entertaining a man who suffered the rigors of slavery, and came looking for his father who, quite likely, also was a slave. Baker spent a silent moment wondering who his father was, and of how he'd respond once he found out.

A glance around the room told Thomas he was a guest in the home of no ordinary Kansas couple. Lining the walls were cabinets filled with china, silver, and crystal, what he assumed were dozens of family photographs under glass, and shelves crowded with books like he'd never seen.

Most of their furniture the Wainwrights gave to the Cumberland Presbyterian Church when they left Tennessee for Kansas, bringing with them only their most cherished possessions. Other items were shipped by freight wagon to Whiskey Flats a few pieces at a time.

Bethy placed on the marble-top table between the men two white china cups, filled them with coffee from a pewter carafe, and busied herself in the kitchen.

Thomas wouldn't be surprised to learn that Bethy was Elizabeth Nelson Wainwright, renowned author of historical novels depicting life in the

South before, during, and after the war. As a slave in the fields of Master Minwell's plantation, Thomas experienced many of the incidents depicted in Bethy's books, and could give first hand, eye-witness accounts of life on the plantation, if invited to do so.

Baker was a science professor at a prominent Tennessee university until Bethy contracted a lung ailment. Her doctors expressed sincere sorrow, but confessed they could do nothing more for her. What would help her most, they advised, was the fresh, clean air of the uncluttered West. Learning of the westward movement, they joined a contingent of people traveling to Kansas, and chose to settle near Whiskey Flats.

Wainwright limped to a blue camel-back sofa, and pointed to a cane-bottomed rocking chair. To Thomas, he said, "Sit over there where it's more comfortable."

Thomas dropped into the rocker, facing the older man who was studying him with an inquisitive smile.

"You say your name is Belt?" Wainwright said.

"Yes, sir. Thomas Belt."

"And you're looking for your father?"

"Yes, sir. My father's name is Harvey Belt."

"Harvey Belt."

Wainwright gave his gray head a thoughtful nod. Surprised to hear the name, he knew who Thomas's father was. He also knew why George Haskell sent Thomas to his door–for a first-hand account of the tragedy.

"Your father was once a slave?"

"Yes, sir, and so was I. Mr. Haskell said you might be able to help me find him."

Baker pinned him with a steady gaze.

"Bethy," he called over his shoulder, using the moment to formulate a response he never thought he'd have to make. "Bring Mr. Belt some more coffee."

Bethy brought the carafe and refilled both men's cups, then left them alone.

"Thomas," Wainwright said, "there's only one way to put this, and I'm sorry to be the bearer of bad news." He paused, watching Thomas's face for reaction that didn't come. "Your father is dead."

That was not the news Thomas hoped to hear. Many days across rigorous miles he struggled since he boarded that steamer at Vicksburg for the five day journey to St. Louis.

He boarded another boat on the Missouri River, arriving finally at a place in Kansas called Wyandotte. At Wyandotte he ran into a former slave named Ezra, whom he recalled from Felix Minwell's plantation.

Ezra arrived in Kansas two years before with a group of freedmen struggling on foot to reach Nicodemus. Ezra looked around, asked questions of people he grew to know, and decided Wyandotte offered greater opportunity for a black man than what he learned about the primitive conditions of Nicodemus. Eventually he was able to build a successful business, doing what he knew best–as a saddler, the same job he performed as a slave on the plantation. Ezra was a wiry, graying man with deep-set eyes. Several years older than Thomas, he wanted to help his young friend on his way.

"You going west?" he asked to Thomas.

"Yes."

"How far west?"

"As far as I have to go to find my father."

"Harvey?" Ezra said. "I never thought he'd leave Mississippi without you and your mama."

"He thought he should come first, and see what Kansas had to offer."

Thomas thought it was not the proper time to mention his father left Mississippi for Kansas while Thomas was in prison. After his escape, Alisha told him of Harvey's plan to come west.

"Do you know where to look?" Ezra asked.

"There's a place called Nicodemus he talked about to my mother. That'll be my first stop."

Ezra knew about Nicodemus. Some former slaves went there and stayed. Others, disappointed in the lack of promise touted by the promoters' fliers, moved on.

"Lots of black folks gone out there and done all right," Ezra said. "Some others didn't do so good. I didn't go because I got acquainted with some folks here who helped set me up in business."

He gazed for a long moment into the questioning eyes of Thomas Belt.

Would it be wise, Ezra counseled himself, to encourage his friend in his quest? Should he urge him, a stranger to the ways of the west, to challenge the rigors of a land where life was rugged, unpredictable as tomorrow, where a black man's chances of finding his father were unlikely. However, Ezra saw in the eyes of Thomas Belt a determination to find his father.

"You'll need a horse," Ezra said. "And supplies."

"I have nothing to pay with."

"Leave that to me. I know you, and I remember your father as an honorable man."

He put out his hand, and Thomas grasped it in a strong handshake. "Come around tomorrow morning," Ezra said, "and I'll get you fixed up. You can pay me when you can pay me."

The next morning, Thomas learned Ezra's word was as strong as his handshake. Off a wooden peg, Ezra lifted a Colt.45 in a leather holster, and a box of cartridges.

"You'll want to take these along," Ezra said, holding them out to Thomas. "They'll protect you from coyotes and rattlesnakes."

Thomas never held such a weapon. He turned the gun over a time or two, and discovered it wasn't as heavy as it appeared. He thanked Ezra for his kindness, and strapped the gun belt around his waist. With a hearty handshake, Thomas climbed aboard the white horse Ezra loaned him.

"Better 'n walkin'," Ezra said.

Thomas set off on his journey with saddlebags full of Ezra's food, and a heart full of hope.

Somewhere west of Wyandotte, Thomas came upon a group of pilgrims from Alabama huddled around a campfire. Seven men, five women–three of them with small babies on their hips–and four older children, all looking forward to the good life in Kansas.

They invited Thomas to join them on their trek

west. Thomas declined. On horseback, he could travel faster.

Up and down rugged hills he rode, around mountains, through fertile valleys, across gorges sculpted by centuries of rain and ravaging winds.

Once, his horse stumbled at a river crossing and flung Thomas head over heels into the water. Thomas struggled to right himself, and fought the rushing current to reach the river bank.

The frantic horse regained footing, kept his head above water, slashing and splashing his way to the river's edge. Finally, Thomas was able to grab the reins and lead the animal ashore.

In the midst of an unknown territory, Thomas battled the devastation of loneliness. He didn't know how far he'd ride to put it behind him, nor whether he'd find a place called Nicodemus. All he knew was what his mother told him, what his father told her. Nicodemus was a settlement of former slaves, refugees from the southern plantations.

Trusting the sun to keep him on course, Thomas's thoughts focused on his father. He tried to put it out of his mind, but it kept cropping up: His father might be dead. Thomas and his mother talked about it, even while trusting it would not be so.

Now, facing the reality of the worst, he was shaken by the words of a total stranger who told him his father no longer lived. And here, staring him in the face, awaiting his response to the revelation, sat the man who must know more about what happened on the night his father was murdered than simply "your father is dead."

"It was some time ago," Wainwright began. "Are

you familiar with an all-black community called Nicodemus?" he asked.

"Yes, sir."

"Harvey once mentioned that he came west," Baker said, "hoping to settle there."

"That was my first stop," Thomas said. "I asked about him at Nicodemus, but nobody could tell me much about my father, except they believed he headed this way."

"I didn't know him well," Wainwright said. "Harvey and I exchanged a few words now and again over a little nip. He told me he left Nicodemus because he was disappointed in what he found there. He talked about wanting to move his wife and son to Nicodemus, but it was hard to make a living in that country.

"He took a job here as a smithy on the Bar T ranch. The night he died, I went to the Bang Tail Saloon for my daily indulgence–Bethy won't allow me to keep the stuff in the house–and I well remember what happened.

"There was some kind of disagreement between your father and a couple of ranch hands. The men challenged Harvey's right to be there. They made some threatening remarks. Harvey took exception to what they said. An altercation broke out, and Harvey gave them both a good thrashing. The sheriff showed up, took a look around, decided Harvey was at fault, and was about to haul him off to jail.

"Your father protested, as he should have, because what happened was not his fault. A couple of ruffians laid hold of Harvey and forced him outside. They looped a noose around his neck and dragged him behind a horse to a tree on the edge of town."

Wainwright's narrative did not include the part about the jeering taunts of the drunks who perforated Harvey's dangling body with gun shots. "After they cleared out," Wainwright said, "I cut him down."

Thomas lowered his head and wiped his eyes. He took the long, hard ride in search of his father. Now this kind, soft spoken southern gentleman described how his father was lynched by a drunken mob.

What was ahead for Thomas now? His mother was dead, his father murdered. Returning to Mississippi would be a fruitless journey. He could go back there, but what kind of life could a former slave live where people still believed slaves had no right to be free, where there was little opportunity to eradicate the stigma of his former life, to lift himself above the degradation of being owned by a white master?

Also, there was the matter of the slave driver he beat to death, for which the law would still be after him. And always in the mind of a black man in Mississippi, free or slave, lingered the fear of being hanged or burned alive by the Klan.

Thomas grew up believing a life of oppression was how things were supposed to be for black people, with nothing to look forward to, except the "promised land" the preachers carried on about when he went to church with his mother.

Peering into the past, Thomas recalled lying awake nights, knowing his father too was sleepless on his straw pallet. Thinking, always thinking, looking for some way to make life better for Alisha, and so his son wouldn't have to "die slavin'."

Three times Harvey tried to escape the plantation. Three times he got as far as the river before the slave patrol dragged him back shackled hand and foot, and turned him over to a jeering slave driver, Bozo Cliff.

Cliff lacerated Harvey's body with a metal-tipped thong, ripping his shirt into blood saturated shreds. He locked Harvey, writhing in pain, in a cage too small for him to stretch his legs, with no food, except for the two biscuits and a cup of water once a day.

Thomas's mother wept bitter tears every time his father was hunted down and brought back.

So did Thomas.

How could he now return to the South, where the Confederates were still fighting the Civil War, believed the south would "rise again"? Freedom was a toothless promise for the four million slaves "freed" by Lincoln's Emancipation Proclamation?

The thought died an early death. Thomas Belt could not return to Mississippi.

Already he could feel the anger stirring in his body, pulling at his consciousness, pushing him toward the need to avenge his father's brutal death. Where would he start?

"Who did it?" Thomas said to Wainwright.

Baker needed a moment to form his answer. It would not be easy, and it must not be quick.

"If you're thinking of retaliating, I understand that," Baker said. "And you have plenty of reason to do so. Those men deserve to be brought to justice.

"And then again, I once heard a wise man say that vengeance is the endeavor of fools. I haven't known you for more than half an hour, but I think I know you pretty well. You, Thomas Belt, are no fool."

Thomas appreciated the sentiment, but was not satisfied with the answer.

"Mr. Wainwright," he said, "do you know who killed my father?"

"I know, but there is nothing to be gained by chasing after a man who has the mind of a child."

"Who was that?"

"One of the Covington boys."

"Cecil?" Thomas said, recalling his encounter with the only Covington he knew.

"Jubal, the oldest," Baker said. "They say he was injured in an accident when he was a young boy, and hasn't been mentally stable since.

"Jubal struck the first blow that sent your father reeling against the wall. That drew taunting approval from the crowd, so Jubal struck again, like a small child repeating the deed to please his parents. I doubt Jubal knew the seriousness of what he did," Wainwright said.

"Does that make him less guilty?" Thomas asked.

Wainwright didn't answer.

"Who else, Mr. Wainwright?"

"A man named Rance Gomer tightened the noose around your father's neck."

"Gomer," Thomas said, as if to himself.

Redford told him Gomer was the one he threw

out of the Bang Tail Saloon.

"Gomer was a drifter Covington took on during the cattle drive," Wainwright said. He drew a hand across his face as if to cleanse his memory of the horrible scene. "The sheriff made no effort to stop it, and nobody took your father's side. They were white and he was black. They needed no other excuse.

"There was a time when I would have stepped in, but that was long ago. Had I intervened, they likely would have hanged me alongside your father. For allowing it to happen, maybe I'm as guilty as the others."

"Who was the sheriff?" Thomas asked.

"Demp Whitton. Jonas Covington owns his badge."

"And Whitton did nothing to stop it?"

"He didn't bat an eye," Baker said.

Thomas let that soak in.

"Can you tell me where my father is buried?" he asked.

Wainwright hesitated. He stroked his chin. "In my back yard."

Thomas cast him a startled look.

Wainwright stood up. "I'll show you," he said. He led the way through the kitchen and out to the back of the house.

Thomas followed a step behind the limping Wainwright.

Bethy looked up from the dough she was kneading at the cabinet, following them with her eyes.

She knew where the men were going. Many

times she dug the weeds around the grave. She didn't know when, nor whether, someone might come seeking answers to the questions Thomas Belt was asking now.

Across a narrow clearing the men walked around beds of daisies and daffodils, to a small mound of dirt. It was hardly noticeable, but Wainwright knew where to find it. Stuck in the dirt at one end of the grave was a crude wooden cross with no name on it.

In the lengthening shadows, Thomas stared at the final resting place of the father he came to find. Hollow as an echo from the distant past, Thomas hardly heard the words of the man who buried his father.

"Bethy planted some flowers around the grave and kept the weeds down," Baker said. "We figured there was little chance anyone would come for the body, but we wanted him to have a decent burial."

Thomas thought about moving his father's remains to Mississippi for burial beside his mother. Would she want that? Maybe. But he decided showing up in Mississippi would be foolhardy. And, where would his father receive better care than in the Wainwrights' back yard?

"I thank you, sir, "Thomas said with a solemn nod. "Would it be all right if I left him–"

He motioned toward the grave.

"Absolutely," Wainwright said, assuring him with a pat on the back. "We'll see it's cared for."

He shook Thomas's hand, and watched him mount up and ride away.

Where could he turn now?

CHAPTER 15

What about Cassie?

Redford glanced at the half dozen poker-faced wranglers and a couple of drummers at the Bang Tail's game tables. Behind the bar, Eden was wringing whiskey drippings from a wet towel when she heard him say, "How's Cassie doing?"

Eden wiped her hands on a white towel, and tossed it under the bar. She took up a bottle and a glass, and led Redford to a table. She placed the bottle on the table, and nodded Redford into the chair facing her.

The whiskey was for him. She saw enough of that during her Jack Claxton captivity. Whiskey never touched her lips. Even so, she sensed Redford's need to talk and would feel more comfortable with a glass in his hand.

"Cassie was pretty shaken up after the fire," Eden said. "She has hardly left her room since, but she's coming around." She uncorked the bottle and poured his glass full. "She said something about going to Topeka to be with some of her people there."

"Topeka? That's quite a way off," he said. "Does she have money for train fare?"

"I don't know."

Redford reached into a pocket, and brought out a roll of bills. He peeled off a few, and handed them to Eden. "Give her this," he said.

"Don't you want to give it to her?"

"She wouldn't take it from me."

"Is this a part of your responsibility of looking after Cassie?"

"You might call it that. I don't know what else I can do. She told me she didn't want me to do anything but leave her alone. She thinks I should have died instead of Cal. She said she never wanted to see me again.

"When do you think she'll be leaving?"

"All I know is she sent a wire back there a few days ago. I don't know whether she's got an answer yet, but I think she's ready to go."

"I hope it works out for her." He took a sip from the glass. "You know I told you before about an obligation I had."

"You mean something besides Cassie?"

"Well, it's a matter I need some help with."

"And what is this one's name?"

"Ashley."

"That sounds like a girlfriend."

"Daughter."

"You have a daughter? Where?"

"San Saba."

"When was the last time you saw her?" Eden said.

"Three years ago."

"How old is she now?"

"She'd be about seventeen," Redford said.

"Is she with her mother?"

"We never got married."

"You never got married?" Eden was aghast. "Did you even think about marrying the mother of your daughter?"

"I thought about it."

"And?"

"I decided against it."

"So," Eden said with obvious disdain, "you've got a teenage daughter you haven't seen for three years, whose mother you never married, and now your guilty conscience is pulling you back, and you can't wait to get out there to– Where was it?"

"San Saba."

"Is that in Kansas?"

"Texas."

"Well, I'm really disappointed in you, Redford. I mean, I've done some pretty raw stuff in my time, but dumping the girl's mother, then running off and leaving her with– Who's in charge of taking care of Ashley?"

"My sister Maude."

"How did it happen?"

"What?"

"You and the girl's mother."

He cast her a sideways glance. "You know how babies happen."

"I mean–were you in love with her?"

"When you're eighteen and drunk, love has nothing to do with it."

"And you were drunk at the time?" Eden said.

"That's what they told me," he said.

"Who told you?"

"Ashley's mother."

"Whose name is?"

"Was. Molly Ingram. She died when Ashley was seven."

"Do you care?"

"l care about Ashley. That was a long time ago."

"And now the repentant father shows up to make sure he totally disrupts the life of his daughter after ignoring her for half her life. Have you been in contact with her? Letters? Wires? Anything?"

Redford gave his head a slow, thoughtful shake. "I'm not proud of what I did," he said.

"Well, I should hope not. You are a totally pitiful human being, Dan Redford, and you should absolutely be ashamed, embarrassed, and totally–unproud–for making no effort to get in touch with your daughter for three years."

"You're right, I was wrong." Colonel Brentwell told him the same thing–with somewhat less contempt.

Redford got up to leave. "Any more questions?" he asked with a sheepish grin.

"You better climb on that horse of yours, beat a fast trail and don't look back till you get to San wherever. And send Ashley a wire before you leave to let her know you're on your way."

"I need to do that." He lifted his glass in a conciliatory salute. "Are we still friends?"

"I'll let you know."

He took a step away, then turned back. "What about that hombre you said was going to kill me?"

"What about him?" she asked.

"Have you seen any more of him?"

"No, have you?"

"He showed up a couple of nights ago."

"You talked to him?" Eden asked.

"It was more like he talked to me."

"And?"

"Like you said, he's got an itch to watch me die. He didn't say why, but he said I'd know when the time comes."

"Does that mean after you're dead?"

"You've got me on that. If you find an answer, I'd like to know what it is."

"Are you worried about it?" Eden said.

"Not as long as I know it's coming."

"Why would he tell you he's going to kill you?"

Redford responded with a 'who-knows' shrug. "That's one I haven't been able to figure out. I've tried to find a reason why he'd want to do in a good ol' boy like me, but I haven't found it yet."

Eden was more concerned than Redford. "Doesn't it bother you that a total stranger comes in here, plants his elbows on my bar, and says he's going to kill you?"

"Well, I'm not ready to be dead yet, but–"

"Has it entered your head to get him first?"

"I've thought about it, but I couldn't do it the

way he's got it laid out. If I decided to kill somebody I'd just do it, and have it done with. It's like he's making a game of it for some reason." He took a deep breath. "You want to step over to Polly's for a bite?"

"No thanks. Tell her howdy," Eden said.

She took the glass and bottle with her back to the bar. "Any idea when your killing might take place?"

Redford looked at her with a grin, half expecting her to continue her tirade. Instead, she slid the glass along the bar to him. He lifted the glass and heard an intrusive voice.

"Well, I'll be damned! If it ain't the hero of the Little Big Horn."

Redford glanced at the back-bar mirror. He saw a burly, slump shouldered man with a round face. Beside him stood a thick jawed stump of a man with a tic to his right eye, and a straw-haired youngster who looked to be about eighteen. All three had pistols laced to their right hips.

"You mean the coward of Little Big Horn, don't you?" said the stump in a hoarse whisper, loud enough for Redford to hear.

"Yeah," jeered the first man. "I guess that's what I do mean. The coward of Little Big Horn."

"Reckon where he was at when the fightin' was goin' on?" the straw haired lad wanted to know.

Watching them in the mirror, Redford shifted the drink to his left hand.

"Why don't you go ask him?" said the man with the tic.

Redford saw Slump Shoulders' lips say to the kid, "Yeah. Why don't you do that, Sandy? We'll back you up."

The straw-haired one adjusted his gun belt to the front. Redford observed his movements in the mirror.

"So, you're the big hero of Little Big Horn?" the youngster sneered to Redford's back. "I say you're the coward of Little Big Horn."

Redford didn't care what the kid thought, nor what he said, but the way he said it sounded like trouble. He stole a glance at Eden behind the bar. She said nothing, but her eyes flashed a caution sign. Those three were up to no good.

"Where was you hidin'," the kid jabbed, "when the lead started flyin'?"

Redford studied the bottom of his glass. Why was there always some snot-nosed kid who had to prove how tough he was?

"My pa died up there," the kid flung at him.

Redford turned for a slow look at the brash youngster. Slight of build, fuzzy chin, half Redford's age. "A lot of people died up there,"

"Too bad you wasn't one of 'em," said the kid.

Redford gave his head a dubious shake. He tried to ignore the young hothead, but it wasn't easy.

"I'm sorry about your pa," he said, "but I didn't kill him."

The tic-eyed one placed a hand on the young man's arm with a whispered warning. "Better back off, kid," he said.

The kid shook it off. "I ain't afraid of him," he spat.

Boot Hill was full of men who weren't afraid. For Redford, there was enough dying at Little Big

Horn, where friends dropped around him with bullets in their heads, or bellies punctured by arrows. Life for him took on a different complexion up there, and he wasn't ready for it to be over.

Escaping the battle with nothing more serious than a bloody shoulder, he made up his mind it was time he hit the trail to Texas to make up for all the years he deprived his daughter of her father. Now, here he was, looking into the flashing eyes of this youngster who blamed him for the death of his father at Little Big Horn.

"I'm gonna kill you, Redford!" the kid flared.

Redford already heard that from somebody else, and wondered if there was a movement afoot to rid the world of anybody named Redford.

"This is for my pa!" the kid screamed, whipping out his gun.

A split second later he lay dead of a shot to the chest from Redford's .44. A handsome young man with an itch for revenge who couldn't wait to get dead, challenging a gun he believed he was faster than.

Redford conceded that the fair-haired kid had a reason to be upset. He lost his father, but had neither the patience nor the skill to back up his threat. The kid's slump shouldered friend flashed his gun, but never got off a shot before Redford planted a slug between his eyes. The stump with the tic tossed his gun aside, threw up empty hands, and made a beeline for the door. His eyes filled of fear he would be next.

Redford, satisfied it was over, holstered his pistol.

"Somebody clear them out of here," Eden said.

A handful of wranglers laid hold of the two bodies and hauled them away.

To Redford she said, "Are you all right?"

He dragged a sleeve across his face. "How right is all right?"

* * * *

Thomas faces trouble

Googoo Pry and Henny Eckles were loafing along the boardwalk in front of Polly Payton's Calico Cafe. The no-good cronies of Rance Gomer looking for something to do to break the monotony of what they were doing already. Eyeing Thomas's mounted approach to Polly's front door, Pry said, "Good lookin' horse you got there, black boy."

Thomas dropped a rein over the rail, and took a step toward the cafe entrance.

He cast Pry a look that said he couldn't care less whether the plug ugly liked his horse.

"Reckon what a feller'd have to pay for a horse like that'n?" Eckles said idly.

"Why, Henny, don't you know?" Pry said. "Them niggers don't pay nothin' for nothin'. If they see somethin' they want, they just up and take it. Ev'body knows they was born stealin'."

Thomas recognized them as the two bullies who were with Gomer when he threw Gomer out of the Bang Tail. Maybe that was why Gomer wasn't with them. Maybe he sent the two hooligans, to needle Thomas into a fight, the job Gomer wouldn't tackle alone. Pausing at Polly's doorway, Thomas aimed a silent stare at the two trouble makers.

"It don't seem right that a nigger's got a fine lookin' horse like that 'n," Pry said, "and me still ridin' that old scruffy ten-year-old mustang, now does it?"

"No, it sure as hell don't," Henny agreed. "I bet you could get a holt o' that purty white'n there for– say–prob'ly next to nothin'. Whatta you think o' that, black man?"

"The horse is not for sale," Thomas said.

"You hear 'at, Henny?" Pry said with a derisive cackle. "Black man say the horse ain't for sale."

Eckles thought that was funny, and added his cackle to Pry's.

"Reckon what he'd do," Pry said, "if we just up and took that horse o' his'n and forgot to pay him for it?"

Thomas made a glaring appraisal of the two hard cases. Alone, neither of them had the grit to face him, but two against one they figured they had an edge if a ruckus broke out.

Thomas didn't want any trouble, but it looked like these two hooligans were trying hard to stir up some. He wouldn't turn his back on it if it came to that.

"Whattaya think o' that idy, black boy?" Pry said.

Belt had already decided what he was going to say, and he said it. "I think you couldn't lick a banty rooster in a bucket of rocks."

Pry made a token move toward the gun on his hip. He saw Redford come out of Polly's.

Pry spread his arms, empty handed. With a smirk, he said, "Maybe some other time."

He stalked away. With a head motion, he told Eckles it was time to go. Eckles fell in behind, and the two roughnecks disappeared into the alleyway behind the building.

"You called it," Redford said to Thomas. "The woods are full of 'em."

* * * *

Cassie takes the train

By noon the next day, Cassie was packed and ready to go. Redford carried her valise and walked her to the train. In view of her recent attitude, Redford was surprised she hadn't mounted a protest. Without a word, Cassie accepted his offer to help with her bag.

It was a silent stroll that took three minutes from the Bang Tail Saloon to the train station. Cassie and Eden hugged and said their goodbyes.

Eden wished her luck. "You can stay at my place any time you want," Eden told Cassie, "for as long as you want."

Cassie didn't make any promises, but thanked Eden for "putting up with me."

The train's engine snorted, and exhaled a cloud of steam, signaling its eagerness to be gone from Whiskey Flats, but it couldn't leave till after Cassie climbed aboard. Cassie hesitated, as if she was not ready to go. She had a sort of soft look on her face that Redford never saw, and was surprised to see it now. Kind of wistful, a striking change from her venomous attitude she scorched him with before.

She didn't say goodbye. She didn't say "thank you for walking me to the train." What she said was, "I guess we won't be seeing each other anymore."

Dan's puzzlement included not knowing how to respond to the first civil word from her since he came back from Little Big Horn.

"Dan?" she asked.

He handed her valise up to the conductor, who carried it up the steps into the coach.

"I guess not," Dan said.

"I want to thank you for looking after me."

"You're welcome."

"Was it only because Cal asked you to?"

"Cassie, I—"

"Does looking after me include coming with me to Topeka?"

Startled by the question, he said, "I don't think that's what Cal meant."

"What do you think he meant?"

"Cal was a good soldier and a good friend. He'd do the same for me."

Her next statement shocked him all the way down to the toes of his boots.

"Dan, what would you think if I told you I'm in love with you?"

The air was heavy.

Redford suddenly had trouble breathing, but the redness creeping into his cheeks was not from the heat. He couldn't believe Cassie would even hint at such a thing. "I don't think it'd be a good idea."

"Why not? I'm a woman, you're a man, both at loose ends. It happens all the time."

"Well, Cassie, you're as pretty a lady as I ever knew," he said. "And I bet there are folks out there who'd stumble all over themselves to be loved by you, but I couldn't do that to Cal."

"Cal's not here anymore."

"Uh-huh. Well, for another thing, I've got a daughter almost as old as you are. Besides that, everything I own is what I'm walking around in."

She pressed a hand to his chest. "I wouldn't expect more than that you let me love you."

He gently removed her hand. "You belong to the man you married," he said.

"I belong to the man who never gave me a second look. I grieved for Cal because he was a good man. I married him because he loved me. I love you."

Heat of the loins was no stranger to Dan Redford. He sometimes struggled to control the demons at work, the ones that could drive a man to drastic consequences. The army quartermaster issued boots, guns, and bullets, but made no provision for female companionship.

Eden was right. It was a long time since he "slept in a good woman's bed."

Had he allowed himself to do so, he could climb aboard that train with Cassie, even though she had stabbed him with accusing eyes, and condemned him unmercifully for not dying instead of Cal.

Still, her confession of love told him a sympathetic smile from him could lead Cassie to read it wrong. He could go with her to Topeka, foot loose, as Cassie said. Except for his need to get to Texas and rescue his daughter from an unsavory situation, he could go with her.

His decision didn't come quickly, but it came. He promised Cal he'd take care of Cassie.

That didn't include taking advantage of her. Nowhere in his makeup dwelt the weakness that would cause him to betray the final request of a dead friend.

"I'm a cowhand, Cassie," he said. "I've been a cowhand since I was twelve years old. Even when I was scouting for the army I wasn't much of a soldier. I was a cowhand who joined the army. I'll never be anything else."

"I don't care what you were," Cassie said. "I know what you are, and I want to be with you. Wherever you go, whatever you do, I want to be there."

"What about Cal? You've acted like it was my fault he died."

"That was because I was afraid if I told you I loved you, you'd turn me away." With tear sparkled eyes, she said, "Now I know you would have."

He surprised himself by placing an arm across her shoulders, pressing her to him.

Cassie was not ready to leave, but the train started heaving forward, and it was time to go. She gave Redford a quick, pleading look, then abruptly turned away. The conductor took her hand and he helped her up the steps into the coach. She chose a seat by the window, and looked back until the image of Dan Redford grew small, and faded in the distance.

He wished her well,
Never again would they meet.

CHAPTER 16

Jonas quizzes his sons

Jonas Covington called his sons together in the front room furnished with heavy oak tables, camelback sofas, and leather-bound chairs. Cora was in charge of that, and all was as she left it when she died five years before.

Jonas didn't invite the boys to sit. They stood in anxious silence, watching their father pace back and forth across the stone floor, shaggy gray head bowed, deep in thought. He rarely called them to that room, except when something important was about to take place—as when he told them their mother was dying. The boys wondered what was on his mind this time.

Jonas struggled with the seriousness of what Whitton told him. Jubal was involved in the Harvey

Belt hanging.

It was a chore convincing himself his oldest son was capable of consciously participating in much of anything, especially something as serious as a lynching. Wrestling with the Thomas Belt matter kept him awake the night before, trying to figure it out, unable to rest until he could satisfy himself as to the strait of it.

Was Jubal involved, or was he only a bystander with no active part in the hanging of Harvey Belt? Whitton told him Jubal struck the first blow, but Jonas had to know for sure. One way or the other, he had to know.

Jonas also wasn't certain whether the stranger who showed up in town–that Thomas Belt fellow– was Harvey's son. But he didn't know he was not his son either. If it turned out he was Harvey's son, as Whitton suspected, Belt would be looking for somebody to blame for his father's death.

There would be bloodshed, and Jonas didn't want it to belong to a Covington, certainly not Jubal. Jonas's mood suddenly swung from puzzled to angry. Covingtons didn't do things like that! They didn't take part in hanging an innocent man, no matter what color he was. His son? His son! His simple minded son–struck the first blow that opened the gate for a whiskey driven mob to circle the neck of a man he didn't know with a hangman's noose.

When he finally found his voice, Jonas stopped pacing and faced the boys with fire in his eyes. "Demp Whitton was out here while you boys were working cattle. He said one of you was involved in the hanging of that black man a while back." He paused to give them time to recall the incident. "Do you remember that?"

Jonas knew which son it was. Whitton told him, but he didn't want to believe the guilty son's name was Jubal. He didn't want it to be Cecil or Nathan either–but Jubal?

Cecil said he remembered it, but he wasn't in town that night.

Jonas's eyes shifted to Nathan. No, he knew it wasn't Nathan. Nathan didn't drink, and never went to the Bang Tail, except to get one of his brothers out of there and bring him home. The last person on earth he'd have thought guilty was Jubal. He hoped Whitton was mistaken.

Dismissing the chance that Nathan or Cecil was the son to whom Whitton referred, Jubal was the only one left. "Jubal?" Jonas said in as calm a voice as he could muster.

Jubal grinned a lot, often when there was nothing to grin about. That was what Jubal did now, and said nothing.

All his life Jonas favored Jubal because he was the oldest. And, he rarely admitted even to himself, that it was because Jubal was mentally weak. He never required as much of Jubal as of the other boys, and never did he inflict upon Jubal the pain of his belt buckle.

Jonas knew Jubal was in on the hanging party. Still, he kept trying to find something that would make it untrue. Hoping he would understand what he was talking about, Jonas settled a hard look on the face of his eldest son.

A man was hanged, and Whitton said Jubal was

a part of it. Jubal said nothing. Where could Jonas go from there? He had to ask. "Jubal, Demp Whitton says you were there the night those people hung that black man–Harvey Belt. Is that right?" He paused, seeking some response that would tell him Jubal had nothing to do with the tragedy. All he got was a foolish grin.

"Dammit, boy!" Jonas couldn't hold it back any longer, even for Jubal. Enough was enough. "If you had anything to do with that hanging, you damn well better be spitting it out right now! Talk to me, boy!"

Jubal was thirty years old, but his mentality stopped growing at age seven. Cringing under Jonas's verbal attack, Jubal's lower lip curled like the little boy whose brain told him what to do.

"Pa, I–" It was Nathan, trying to inject some calm into the situation.

Jonas ignored him. He spewed his venom upon Jubal whose guilt he could not believe, but he was the one Whitton named as an accomplice.

All his life Nathan believed Jubal was favored by his father because of his mental weakness. Now, it occurred to him Jonas denied the affliction of his eldest son, rendering him less than a man. In the eyes of his father, Jubal was a blight on the proud Covington name. And Jonas harbored no respect for any man, son or stranger, without the grit to stand up for himself.

Nathan never suffered the pain of his father's lashing. He cringed now, as Jonas ripped off his belt and began flailing away at Jubal's back with the buckle end. Jubal was a bigger man than his father, but displayed no resistance to the abuse.

Cecil stood apart, as fearful of his father as was his brother Jubal. Numerous times had he received the same treatment, feeling the pain Jubal was now going through. But never had he seen Jonas take the belt to Jubal. He was frightened, as if witnessing the brutality of a man he didn't know.

Jubal appealed to Nathan with a pitiful look that said, "Make him stop hitting me."

Nathan did. "Pa," he said, as Jonas laid the belt on Jubal. "Pa!"

Jonas stopped swinging, the belt in mid-air, poised for another blow to Jubal's already blood streaked back. He cast a squint-eyed glare at Nathan as he might view a total stranger. For too many years Nathan stood silently by, watching as Jonas laid the belt on Cecil for whatever reason he thought he deserved it. Nathan didn't approve of the beatings his father inflicted upon his younger brother, but he never questioned Jonas's authority to discipline his son.

Still, Nathan, who always obeyed his father's instructions, didn't dispute what Jonas deemed the proper way to handle a given situation. In spite of what Jubal did, Nathan believed the lashing was uncalled for–lacerating Jubal's broad back, shredding his shirt till it was sticky with blood.

With a scowl at Nathan, Jonas held the belt ready to strike Jubal again. "Don't hit me, daddy," Jubal whimpered. He threw up an arm to protect himself from further abuse. Eyes flooded with the tears of a seven-year-old, Jubal moved beyond his father's reach.

Jonas lowered the belt, eyes shooting darts at Nathan, puzzled that his usually unobtrusive second son interfered, for never before had he done so. The mild mannered Nathan, Jonas seethed with a vengeful glare...another one who didn't have the guts to stand up to me.

"You hit Jubal one more time," Nathan said calmly to his father, "and I'll kill you."

Jonas's face was a mask of disbelief. "What's that you say?"

"You heard me, Pa. I've stood by long enough without saying anything. Cecil didn't deserve all the lickings you gave him. And I don't think Jubal does either, no matter what he's done."

Jonas's disbelief turned to rage. For a moment he said nothing, glared at Jubal with utter disgust, and took a threatening step toward Nathan as if to use the belt on him. "Why, you sniveling pup!" Jonas railed at Nathan. "You always was short on grit."

Nathan stood his ground. "I'll do it, Pa," He drew the gun laced to his right thigh. "You've laid the leather on Cecil for the last time, and we don't know for sure what Jubal did."

To Jubal, Jonas said, "Are you gonna stand there and let your whining little brother put a bullet in me, boy?"

Jubal tried to grin, but it was more like a painful sob. All the pain would allow him to do was cast a terrified look at Jonas. Jubal pleaded with Nathan to rescue him from further lashing.

"Jubal!" Jonas shouted, but his eldest son made no move. Jonas stood for a moment, eyes narrowed to fiery slits.

Nathan wondered whether Jonas might make a move for his gun, hoping he wouldn't. He didn't want to shoot his father, but he would if it came to that.

Jonas flung the belt aside, turned his back on Nathan with an irritable wave of his hand, dismissing Nathan's threat as nothing more than an annoyance. "You never was worth a hiccup in a hailstorm!" He sneered at Nathan.

Jonas took a few steps away, wheeled around with his hand full of revolver, and fired a shot. Nathan fell backwards, arms wrapped around his stomach, red with spurting blood. Jonas's eyes focused on his fallen son, as though someone else fired the shot that felled him.He didn't believe Nathan would shoot him, but his middle son–the one who never did anything wrong–defied his father in the presence of his brothers.

"You would shoot your own father?" Jonas said to Nathan, incredulous.

Nathan's lips moved, but only a hoarse whisper emerged. "I–I didn't want to, Pa," he said. "I swear on mama's grave, I didn't want to shoot you."

"Not on your mama's grave!" Jonas roared. "You best never swear on your mama's grave!"

"Pa," Nathan gasped. "Pa!"

Jonas's piercing eyes shifted from Nathan to Cecil. "Ride into town and tell Doc Bowman to get out here as fast as he can. We won't move your brother till he gets here."

Cecil dashed from the house, hit the saddle of his mare tethered at the front door, and took off toward town at a hard gallop.

CHAPTER 17

The killer thinks it over

With a sycamore sprout, Emitt Coldwater stirred the fire. He could have slept in a soft bed at Mrs. O'Rourke's again, but there would be people there, and he didn't want anyone around. His mind was cluttered with things he had to work out. He needed time to himself, with no distractions.

He kicked himself for not having it out with Redford when he had the chance. He could have shot him dead where he stood. But, had he shot from the dark, Redford wouldn't know who did him in, nor why.

Coldwater's plan was to look Redford in the eye, dare him to draw, then wipe him out with the lightning flash of his Colt .44–the last thing Redford would see.

Angry with himself, Emitt tossed another stick of wood onto the red hot embers. Things hadn't played out the way he planned. Boasting to that bartender woman, he didn't tell her why he was going to kill Redford. She warned him that trying to kill Redford was not a good idea. She said Redford would kill him "before you clear leather." Was that what froze Emitt's hand when he saw Redford face-to-face that night?

On the long ride from San Saba, Coldwater worked at convincing himself that Redford was just a man, who put his boots on one foot at a time, the same as everybody else. He hadn't faced a kill or be killed situation. He never killed a man, and didn't want to kill this one, but his body ached for Ashley who told him "Over my dad's dead body."

Now, with time to think about it, he wasn't certain she meant it the way it came out. It didn't make sense that she'd want her dad dead so she could marry some guy without a job, who didn't know how to do much of anything besides cut fire wood. There were times when he hired out as a wrangler, but that didn't pay much, and it wasn't steady work.

What if Ashley was only making a joke? Even so, crazy in love with Ashley, he heard it as any crazy in love man might–without thinking of the consequences. Nagging questions, for which he found no answers, bounced off the walls of his mind. *What if?* became a major factor he hadn't counted on. What if Ashley was only joking? What do I do now? Redford thinks I'm here to kill him. I told him I was going to.

Even maybe popped up, confusing his thinking. He expected the woman behind the bar to tell Redford he was going to kill him, maybe the threat of a face-off in the middle of Parker Street would cause Redford to high-tail it out of town, and he wouldn't have to do it. What if Redford didn't scare off? What if he should decide to kill him first?

Coldwater's plan took an unexpected turn for the worse. Redford was more of a man than he anticipated. Doubts about what he came to do were clouding Emitt's thinking.

What if he backed out? What would that say to Ashley? He was a coward? He didn't have the guts to face her father in a showdown with the future of his daughter at stake? He didn't want her badly enough to do whatever it took to get her? On the other hand, what would he tell her if he went through with it, and came out alive?

Hi, hon! I killed your dad. Now will you marry me? Would she still want him? What if she refused to marry him because he killed her father?

Emitt tried not to consider a death-dealing slug plunging into his own head. What would he gain by killing Redford if it caused him to lose Ashley? Had he ridden hundreds of lonely miles from San Saba to Whiskey Flats, maybe to get himself killed because of some dumb notion that he could outdraw a gun-wise man like Redford? He'd pictured Ashley's father as some worn out old puncher with one eye and a stooped back, whose gun hand long since went limp. His brief encounter with Redford, even on a dark street, told him he misjudged the man who stood between him and the girl he wanted.

Angry at himself for being such a fool, Emitt flung another stick on the dying embers. How long and lonely would be the ride of a coward with a raw sausage for a gun hand, slinking back to Texas?

* * * *

Nathan is dead

By the time Doc Bowman arrived at the Circle C ranch in his one-horse buggy half an hour before sundown, Nathan lost so much blood he drifted into unconsciousness. Bowman instructed Cecil and Jubal to move their brother to a bedroom, where he tried to make him comfortable.

Bowman, a tall, hollow chested man of sixty-nine, cared for the Covington family for as long as Jonas could remember, and laid Cora to rest when she could no longer breathe.

The doctor inspected Nathan's wound, exposing a gaping gash from where the blood gushed. He called for soft cloths and hot water to swab the wound. Cecil brought them.

Finally, the old doctor gave his hairless head a sorrowful shake. "I came as soon as I could," he said to Jonas, "but there's nothing more I can do for your son." He pulled the sheet over Nathan's head. "I'm sorry."

Jonas placed a hand on the doctor's shoulder, as if he understood. "You did what you could."

"How did it happen?".

Jonas studied the faces of his sons. Jubal's eyes were filled with tears. Cecil wiped his eyes with the back of his hand. Jonas decided this was not the time to explain to the doctor what took place between himself and his dead son—whom he shot and killed in a fit of rage. All Jonas could muster was a sad shake of his shaggy gray head.

Doc Bowman responded with a sympathetic nod.

Jonas asked him to take Nathan's body into town and prepare it for burial. Bowman said he would. He watched the boys place their brother's body in his buggy. Climbing onto the driver's seat, Bowman flicked the lines, and the horse moved out.

Cecil and Jubal, with arms across each other's shoulder, followed with tear-filled eyes the departing buggy bearing the body of their dead brother. They didn't take their eyes off it until the buggy disappeared in the thickening shadows that told them night was not far behind. Neither of them looked at their father.

CHAPTER 18

Independence Day in San Saba

San Saba was five years old when the morning of July 4, 1859, dawned bright and clear. It was perfect for the celebration planned by the city fathers–and one aggressive city mother–for observing the eighty-third anniversary of the Declaration of Independence. Planning for the activities began weeks before when Mayor Jessup Catlin huddled with a few prominent citizens and asked them to put the program together.

One of those with whom he huddled was Pearly Mae Witherspoon. Pearly Mae was old, skinny, and flat chested. The mayor consulted Pearly Mae because he respected the memory of her late father, one of the early settlers in San Saba. A few years later the town became recognized as "the pecan capital of the world," proudly producing enough nuts to merit the distinction, the most prominent of whom was Pearly Mae Witherspoon.

Mrs. Witherspoon exerted her familial privilege, assuming control of the committee before any of the other members could protest. That was not what the mayor had in mind, but by the time he found out what was happening it was too late. Pearly Mae's was the only oar in the water. Other members of the group made no effort to oppose her, for, according to Pearly Mae's appraisal, none of them knew anything about planning a celebration of greater magnitude than a Saturday night smoke-in with beer and cigars.

Pearly Mae decreed there would be no boring speeches on this special day unless she made them—which she, thankfully, decided not to do. It was a bold maneuver on her part, since the recently elected mayor had no opportunity to appeal to his constituents for their votes in the next election, so far unscheduled.

In addition to which, the citizens had no time to find out how well the mayor would perform in his newly acquired official capacity, nor that he may not even be qualified for his first term let alone a second one.

Even so, the mayor was justifiably miffed because he was banished by Pearly Mae to the darkness. However, he dared not express his disappointment lest she wage a campaign of recall, which more than likely would have cost him the coveted mayorship. Sadly, Catlin labored for weeks over the wisdom-and-patriotism-filled speech he hoped to share with the gathering on the Fourth of July.

Barging ahead, Pearly Mae proceeded with plans of her own, "laid out by the committee" for the big day. Activities included fireworks; kick ball and hopscotch for the kids; food prepared by the women's circle of the Methodist Church; red, white, and blue banners for decorating store fronts and doorways of homes. They even adorned the bridles of horses ridden or driven in the parade down Main Street.

There would be no consumption of alcoholic beverages, nor smoking of pipes, nor smelly cigars during the observance. The cloths covering the serving tables on both sides of the street would be red, white, and blue.

Editor Trussell gave Pearly Mae's program a front page spread in his San Saba News. Trussell and his prim British wife Priscilla migrated from England to Texas two years before. Their settling in the God forsaken wilderness of west Texas–"do they serve tea there?"–mystified friends, neighbors and total strangers on both sides of the water.

The answer was no tea, but the Trussells soon became active members of the community. Trussell's News photo of Pearly Mae exposed her false teeth in a broad smile, portraying her as the organizer of the celebration. Pearly Mae ate that up, frosted with false humility.

Everybody did as she told them, and the day turned out to be a rousing success. Pearly Mae modestly accepted accolades for "all the time and effort devoted to planning such a wonderful celebration." She relished the attention, with no recognition of her colleagues' contributions to plans for the festivities, none of which she considered.

Pearly Mae would have been appalled had she known some of the younger people violated without apology her no-drinking decree. At the close of the festive day, at least two of them–a teen aged boy and a weakly reluctant young lass–chose to cap off Independence Day in the hay loft of the local livery stable. Wrapped in each other's arms, young Dan Redford and Molly Ingram passionately arranged their bodies in what Mrs. Witherspoon would abhor as "a compromising position."

"No, Danny, you're drunk," Molly said.

"Maybe," Danny said.

"We shouldn't be doing this," Molly said with scarcely breath enough to voice the mild protest.

"You want to quit?" said young Dan.

"Oh, no! I want it!" said the squirming Molly. She feverishly offered her bare bottom in the hay while Danny struggled to get his pants down. "I want all of it!" she said.

All of it she got, and nine months later she got a small bundle of red-faced, squalling baby girl conceived in the hay loft of the livery stable on the Fourth of July, 1859. Her name was Ashley.

Even now Ashley stole away, as she had in her growing up years, to her be-alone place in the mulberry tree south of her Aunt Maude's house on the banks of the San Saba River. When she was little, her daddy built the "tree house" consisting of half a dozen pine planks spanning two limbs secured with rope.

As a young girl, she spent many hours sharing the joys and sorrows of the characters in a favorite book. At seventeen she still escaped to her secret sanctuary, seeking privacy to think about important things, like how far it was from San Saba, Texas, to Whiskey Flats, Kansas. That's where her father was the last time she heard from him. And, how long would it take to get there if she started now?

She also sought the privacy of her tree house to avoid the clumsy advances of her Uncle Sid. Sid McGuire was a heavy set, big-boned man with pale eyes and a stubble of chin whiskers. Sid was lazy, lewd, licentious, and married to Ashley's Aunt Maude. Ashley hated him.

Her father was gone for months at a time on cattle drives to Kansas. He later took a job wearing a deputy sheriff's badge in Whiskey Flats. When her father signed on as a scout for the cavalry, he stayed away even longer.

From the age of seven, she saw little of him. That was when her mother Molly died of the fever. After the funeral, her father arranged for Ashley to "stay with your Aunt Maude until I get settled." By the time Dan was able to make it back to Texas, Ashley was twelve years old. That was when he told her Kansas was "not a good place for a young girl to grow up."

Since Molly died, Redford twice took the long ride back to San Saba to visit his daughter. The last time was when she turned fourteen.

Ashley detested her abusive Uncle Sid. When he was drunk, which was often, many times had she slapped away his fumbling hands. As she grew older, Sid's advances became more frequent and more repulsive.

"Come sit on Uncle Sid's lap," he would say with a lascivious leer.

When Ashley resisted, he forced her onto his lap and fondled her breasts and thighs until they hurt. Aunt Maude was decent enough, but rarely displayed a willingness to oppose Sid's abusive treatment of her niece. Once in a while, when Ashley fought to free herself, Aunt Maude rescued her by demanding that Sid "get some more wood for the fire."

But, for the most part, Maude's eyes remained closed, and her protests silent. Fearing retribution from her sleazy husband, Maude usually found things to keep her busy in other parts of the house.

The only time Ashley drew a comfortable breath was when Sid was away, often for weeks at a time. Aunt Maude didn't tell her where he went–if she knew–nor what he did while he was gone. Sid seemed always to have plenty of money when he got back from wherever he went, though Ashley couldn't recall a time when he hit a lick of work.

While Sid was gone she thought of running away, but Aunt Maude pleaded with her not go, fearing Sid would beat her again if he didn't find Ashley there when he returned. Hoping it would be enough to get her to Kansas when she got the chance to get away, Ashley tucked into a small leather pouch the money her father sent over time.

Small-boned with fine facial features, and silky yellow hair bouncing off her narrow shoulders, Ashley longed to escape the unsavory environment in which she was forced to grow up because she had no other place to go. She spent private time wondering about Whiskey Flats, Kansas. Where was it? How far away was it, and would her father still be there when she arrived?

Emitt Coldwater, she sometimes pondered, might be her most promising escape from her lecherous Uncle Sid. Emitt kept pressing her to marry him, but she wasn't sure spending the rest of her life with him was what she wanted. He was nice enough, good looking, with dark hair and a jovial manner, and fun to be with, but some of his friends were not. A couple of them were involved in cattle rustling, and one of them served time for it.

In a letter to her father, Ashley mentioned a "friend of mine, Emitt Coldwater." She told him she and Coldwater had kept company for a while. "He's kind of rough cut and rowdy–but he treats me nice, and keeps after me to marry him. I told him 'over my dad's dead body.' (Ha!)." She ended the letter, as always, with "When will I see you again?"

Redford read the letter, read it again, re-folded it, and tucked it in a shirt pocket. She didn't say so outright, but what he read between the lines told him Ashley was miserable in the home of his sister and her abusive husband. Reason enough for him to stop lolly-gagging around Whiskey Flats and hit the trail to Texas.

He wasn't much good at letter writing, but he sent Ashley money once in a while, assuring her he loved her, and he would "get out there to see you" when he could.

The words of Colonel Brentwell flashed across

his mind: Three years is a long time for a daughter to wait for a visit from her father.

Redford knew how lucky he was to ride away from Little Big Horn. He decided it was time he kept the promise to himself and headed for San Saba. But then, there was Thomas Belt. Redford knew he would need help with whatever he made up his mind to do about the hooligans mob that lynched his father.

Added to that was the puzzling matter of the man who broadcast his intention to kill him. For what reason had he made up his mind to do that, and when was he likely to try? Everything takes time, he mused, asking himself which of the problems stood at the head of the line.

Not only because of Ashley was he getting serious about heading southwest, but for himself, to make up for denying himself the pleasure of spending time with his daughter. Reminded of Eden's flare-eyed raking over, he told himself it was time he hotfooted it back to Texas.

Rising with the sun, he headed for the Mercantile and packed his saddlebags with beef jerky, coffee, beans, and tobacco for the trip to San Saba. His overnight self-counsel made it clear he wasn't a very good father to a daughter who deserved better. Little Big Horn influenced his decision, and Eden Fletcher let him know in no uncertain terms he better get cracking.

The plan was set, and he was anxious to get on the way. It would be a long, hot ride. But, if he didn't go now, there was no telling what might happen to prevent his making the trip at all. If he was ever going to make any kind of life for himself with Ashley, he better do it now.

Not for many years had he called San Saba home, and he gave little thought to settling there now. It might make sense though, at this time in her life, and his, to encourage Ashley to come back with him to Kansas where his roots grew deep. He didn't mention it to Eden, and likely wouldn't, unless the matter came up between them, but he'd thought about making some kind of life with the lady saloon owner. He doubted she would bring it up, and probably would laugh at him if he did.

A place to call home was something he didn't have, and hadn't for a long time. He never knew the good feeling of someone welcoming him home after a hard day's ride. It was just a thought. But it could happen.

When he told Eden about his plan to hit the trail to San Saba, she congratulated him for doing the right thing, although it "took you a hell of a long time to start acting like a daddy."

"I didn't know how to be a daddy," he said.

Eden issued strict orders that he "send Ashley a wire on your way out of town so she'll know you're on the way."

"I will," he said.

He spotted Thomas Belt at the table in the corner. With an "excuse me" nod to Eden, he stepped over there. He hadn't seen Belt for a while, and wondered how the search for his father was going.

"I found him," Thomas said.

"That's good."

"Not so good. He was in Baker Wainwright's back yard."

"In his back yard?"

"That's where Wainwright buried him after he cut him down."

Redford heard about the lynching of Harvey Belt, but knew nothing of the details.

"After that bunch of drunks hung him," Thomas said.

Redford liked Thomas Belt. He suspected not many people in town would consider themselves his friends. From the dour look on Thomas's face, and the somber tone of his voice, Redford sensed something serious was about to take place in Whiskey Flats.

Dan wanted to stick out his hand and say, "Count me in," but he was packed up and ready to head for Texas. Whatever the black man had in mind, Redford thought, would put a damper on when he'd leave, if he volunteered to stand with him. His overactive huncher, however, kept yelling at him: Thomas will need help getting it done. He hadn't yet wired Ashley he was coming, so she wouldn't be disappointed if his departure was delayed.

"I went to see the preacher," Belt said, motioning Redford to a chair at the table. "I figured if anyone would tell me the truth, he would. Haskell put me onto a man named Wainwright. Wainwright was there–here, in the Bang Tail Saloon–the night they hung my father."

Redford gave his head a dubious shake. "Why would they hang your father?"

"He was black, and an ex-slave," Thomas said.

"Like me."

"That's no reason to hang a man."

"For some people it was. Wainwright saw the whole thing. The way he explained it, three people did most of the damage. The ringleader was Gomer."

Redford nodded. "The one you threw out of here."

"Wainwright says Gomer put the noose around my father's neck. Another one was Jubal Covington."

"Jubal?" A child in a man's body? "What did he have to do with it?"

"Mr. Wainwright says my father got the best of a couple of wranglers in some kind of ruckus. The sheriff tried to arrest him, and my father protested. That's when Jubal knocked him against the wall."

"You said there were three of them."

"That's what he said. A man Wainwright says had nothing to do with the hanging, but could have stopped it and didn't. The sheriff."

"Demp Whitton." Redford was surprised.

"He didn't turn a hand to slow it down."

It took some doing for Redford to digest the significance of what he was hearing. Dan respected Whitton as a lawman, even though everybody knew Covington had the sheriff in his hip pocket. Jubal was a Covington, and Gomer was a Covington hand. Was that reason enough for Whitton to sit it out?

"So, what are you thinking?" Redford said.

Thomas raked a hand across his chin, eyes locked on Redford's.

"It sounds like you aim to go after them," Redford said. He knew there was more to be said, and waited for Thomas to say it.

"I'm no gunman," Thomas said with a wry grin. "Slaves don't have much time for practicing, and snakes and coyotes don't shoot back. I've been working on my aim, though, like you said. I talk tough sometimes, but you know talk without something to go with it can get a man dead." He sipped at his coffee. "I heard Gomer skipped town after that scuffle with me. I don't know, but if he did, I'll have to go after him."

"How about Jubal Covington?" Redford looked away, as if searching for answers that must be out there some place. "Jubal's a seven-year-old boy in a man's body."

"Wainwright told me. I'll ask you the same question I asked him: Does that make him less guilty?"

"You'll have to ask somebody smarter than I am about that."

"I'd have to go through his father and brothers to get to Jubal."

"There are only two Covington brothers now. Nathan, the middle one, is dead."

"Dead?"

Thomas remembered the mild mannered Nathan from his set-to with his brother Cecil. "I hadn't heard," he said. "How did it happen?"

"The way I get it," said Redford, "Nathan and Jonas got into it about something, and Jonas shot him."

Life was getting complicated for the survivor of

the Little Big Horn. He promised Cal Courtney he'd look after Cassie. The last thing he did for her was carry her bag to the train, to make sure she got safely on her way to Topeka. He didn't feel right about the way he and Cassie parted, but he couldn't think of a better way to do it.

Now, he had to deal with another bump in the road. Thomas hadn't asked, but Redford knew the former slave wouldn't get far alone with his plan to avenge his father's death. Added to that was the threat of getting himself killed by some stranger with a grudge he couldn't identify. Redford couldn't stack things up in any particular order, but all of them had to be dealt with.

The thought was interrupted when he heard Demp Whitton call his name. He turned toward the door and saw Demp motioning to him with a worried look on his face. Redford cast Belt a departing nod and headed that way. He could tell the sheriff was in a frenzy.

Redford matched him stride for stride till they reached the sheriff's office. Whitton led the way inside.

Dan said, "What's up?"

"Trouble. We need to talk."

* * * *

Goodbye, Nathan

It took three days for Doc Bowman to get back to the Covington ranch with Nathan's body prepared for burial. Mid-afternoon the following day, a few neighbors gathered to pay their respects to the young man they knew as quiet and unobtrusive.

The burial plot was on a hillside beyond what once was Cora's vegetable garden north of the house. The men removed their hats, and the women–in gingham, ankle-length dresses and sun bonnets–sobbed and sniffled into tear-stained handkerchiefs.

Pastor Haskell told what he knew about the life of Nathan Covington, including his attendance at Sunday morning church services. Just the Sunday before, Nathan sat on the pew with the Wainwrights, and passed the offering plate when it was time.

At the graveside. Haskell recited the Twenty-Third Psalm, and closed with a plea to the Lord to "receive this young man into your loving arms and give him rest."

Nathan's casket was lowered into the open grave next to his mother's. The last shovel of dirt was tossed onto the grave by Jonas. He was heard to murmur, "I'm sorry son. I'm so sorry."

The men pressed their hats on. The women wiped their eyes, whispering condolences to Jonas and the boys as they turned away. Cecil and Jubal stood for a long time, staring at the mound of dirt from which their brother would not rise. The mourners climbed into their buggies, mounted horses, and turned away in silent respect.

Already, the mind of Jonas Covington was spinning. On the way to the house, he said to Cecil, "Find Rance Gomer."

* * * *

We've got trouble

Whitton tossed his hat at a wall peg, watched it catch, and dropped into the captain's chair behind his desk. He motioned Redford into a straight backed chair facing him, and Dan eased onto it.

The sheriff leaned forward, pinning Redford with an anxious look. "Belt had that run-in with Cecil, and Jonas blames Thomas for causing him to shoot Nathan."

Redford gave his head an odd shake. "That makes no sense."

"I know that, and you know that, but Jonas is hell bent on spilling blood because of it. I don't know how much you know about it, Dan, but a while back a bunch of wild-eyed rowdies hung a black man named Harvey Belt. I know now that Harvey was Thomas's father."

"I heard about it," Redford said, "but I wasn't around when it happened."

"I was there that night," Demp said. "Rance Gomer looped a noose around Harvey's neck and dragged him down the street to a tree outside of town. Jubal Covington was in on it too. Now this man turns up looking for his father. Jonas is breathing fire because he's afraid Belt will be coming after Jubal. I know Jonas, Dan. When he makes up his mind, he'll move before Belt figures out what's happening. I made a mistake," the sheriff went on with a sad shake of his head, "for not trying to stop it."

"So, why are we talking about it now?"

"I owe Jonas Covington. He's paid my wages for twelve years because the county had no money for it."

That was no secret, but Redford nodded.

"I'm grateful to him for that," Demp went on, "but what he's got in mind for dealing with Thomas Belt is hard to swallow. What Belt did to Cecil, the kid brought on himself. And Jonas's shooting Nathan was nobody's doing but his own."

"I hear what you're saying, Demp," Redford said, "but I haven't figured out where I fit in."

Whitton reached into a drawer, brought out a silver star, and slid it across the desk.

"I want you to pin that on, Dan," he said. "I told you when you left for the army your deputy's job would be waiting for you when you got back if you wanted it. You haven't told me what your plans are, but now I'm asking. You don't owe me anything, but you were the best damn deputy a man ever had, and I need you to wear it again." Demp shook his head. "I don't have the stomach for that kind of warfare anymore."

Dan said, "I'll think about it."

"You better think fast," Demp said. "All hell will bust loose when Jonas makes his move. There's no way to tell when that might be, but he'll bring plenty of fire power with him. Jonas knows I don't have the backbone of a hog fart in a tornado anymore, but when he sees you with that badge, it might cause him to think a little longer about whether to declare war. Either way, I don't want to be the only man facing his guns when it happens."

The sheriff paused for a deep breath. "I've made some dumb moves in my time, some things I maybe should've done different." He waved a hand as if to dismiss the subject. "You think I don't know I've been Covington's sheriff for twelve years, Dan? I do know it. I've taken his money, I've taken his abuse, and I've done what he said, because I'm not the man I once was."

Redford agreed with that. "Nobody is."

"You're the only help I can count on in this town," Demp said, "and I've got to keep Covington from running roughshod, throwing a rope around Thomas Belt's neck, and swinging him from a tree like they did Harvey."

Redford had nothing against Covington, but he respected Whitton. He didn't want to leave the sheriff standing alone against Jonas and what other guns he might have to face. Redford made no commitment to Thomas, but he couldn't turn his back on him.

Thomas's plan included going after Gomer and Jubal. Now, the sheriff asked Redford to pin the badge on, carry the law in Whiskey Flats, and maybe flect a bloody fight between Belt and the Covington outfit–a fight Thomas couldn't win by himself.

"I'm going to lock Belt in my jail, and hope this thing blows over," the sheriff said. "I don't want to see him die at the hands of a hot headed lynch mob like his daddy did. I owe him that much."

Thomas would be safe in jail unless Jonas found a way to tear it down, and he might. Whitton would make a stand, but Covington's gunmen could ride over Demp to get to Belt and haul him out of jail, or even string him up on the spot.

Redford was anxious to get out of town to Texas. But, he counseled himself, I've waited this long, I guess I can wait a while longer, till after this is settled.

"I don't need the badge," he said to the sheriff. "I'll stand with you."

* * * *

Find Rance Gomer

Cecil pulled up at the bar in the Deep Six Saloon and waited for the burly, heavy bearded bartender to turn around and look at him so he could ask him what he wanted to know.

The bartender, Bump Cauley, saw Cecil come in, but was in no hurry to acknowledge his presence. Bump looked up from polishing whiskey glasses in the shiny metal tub under the bar long enough to greet Cecil with a scowl.

"I'm Cecil Covington," the boy said.

"I know who you are."

"Jonas Covington's boy."

"I know that too," Bump said. "Everybody in the county knows you're Covington's kid. You don't have to advertise it." The disgruntled Cauley had little regard for Jonas Covington.

One of those settlers whose cattle perished because Covington posted guards to keep them off his grass and water, Cauley couldn't care less whose kid Cedcil was, least of Jonas Covington's. Forced out of the cattle business, Cauley took the job tending bar at the Deep Six.

"What are you doing here, kid?" he asked

"Rance Gomer."

No love was lost between himself and Covington, but Cauley thought even less of the obnoxious Gomer. When he parked his backside on a chair at a poker table in the Deep Six, all Gomer did was look for trouble, and he usually found it.

"Yeah? What about Gomer?" Cauley said.

"I'm looking for him," Cecil said.

Cecil swept a glance at the card players at the game tables shooting glares at him. More than likely they knew who he was and who he belonged to, with nothing good to recall of their dealings with Jonas.

"My pa wants to talk to him," Cecil said to Cauley.

"What about?"

"Pa's got a job for him."

Cauley picked up a towel, in no hurry. He casually began wiping whiskey drippings off the bar. Anything Jonas Covington was up to, Cauley didn't want any part of.

"What kind of job?" he asked.

"That's what my pa wants to talk to him about."

"Gomer's ain't too work brittle," the bartender said, "unless he can do it sitting down. He was here a while ago, but I don't know if he still is."

Bump took a look around the room. The gamblers went back to their cards. He saw no one who cared what was going on at the bar between himself and the Covington boy.

Cauley moved his eyes, and cocked his head toward a door at the back of the room.

Cecil cast him a questioning look.

Bump responded with a stare that Cecil read as a sign Gomer was in the back room. Because of Gomer's explosive temper, the bartender didn't want him to know he told the Covington kid where he was. He offered Cecil a nod.

Cecil stared back.

Cauley didn't blink.

Cecil wound his way between the tables, eased open the door to the back room, and stepped inside.

"Well, lookee who's here," Gomer sneered. "The tough kid from the Bang Tail Saloon. I hear you scared the hell outta that black man, and he high-tailed it plum outa town."

Googoo Pry sat to Gomer's right, Henny Eckles on his left. In the middle of the table was a pile of coins. Pry and Eckles snickered, and left the talking to the brash Gomer.

"You coming or going?" Gomer said to Cecil with a derisive grin.

"Pa sent me to look you up," Cecil said.

"Well, you're looking at me."

Gomer checked his poker hand and tossed it onto the pot. "I'm out," he said. "You say your pa sent you?"

"That's right."

"Why would he do that?" Gomer wanted to know.

"He wants to talk to you."

"Well, now ain't that something?" Gomer said to

his cronies. "The whole time I rode for his brand, Jonas Covington never said shit to me, except to holler at me for something he wanted done. "Why do you reckon he wants to talk to me now?"

"He knows about your run-in with the black man," Cecil said.

"Yeah?"

"That's what he wants to talk to you about."

"Uh-huh. That the same one you run outa town?"

"He's still around."

"Well, I tell you what, little Covington kid," Gomer sneered, "you go back out there and tell that old devil that if he wants to talk to me, I'll be right here. He can come tell me what he wants to gab about, instead of sending his boy to carry the word."

"That's what I'll tell him," Cecil said, moving away.

"You do that. And tell him if it's got something to do with taking care of that black man, he better have a damn good reason before he counts me in."

"I will."

* * * *

Jonas rages

Jonas Covington never allowed himself to be pushed around by anybody. If there was pushing to be done, he was the one who could be counted on to do it. He pushed those nesters off his grass and water. He pushed his sons to do more work than they knew they could do. He pushed Demp Whitton to do something to justify his wages. And he pushed county officials for legal favors because he was paying for the only law in the county.

Now, Rance Gomer conjured up the gall to demand that Jonas–Jonas Covington!–stoop to Gomer's gutter level, dealing with him instead of sending his boy to plead for the opportunity to tell him what he wanted.

For two days Jonas ranted in a blue-veined rage, swearing at everybody and nobody, entreating the power of the Almighty to damn Rance Gomer to hell. Jonas had no respect for Gomer as a human being. He wasn't even much of a hand with cattle when he rode for the Circle C. Jonas took him on only because in the middle of the roundup good wranglers were hard to come by.

But now he needed a gun hand, and Gomer was the only man he knew besides himself who held a grudge against Thomas Belt. Jonas was betting Gomer would be eager for a chance to get even with Belt for throwing him out of the Bang Tail Saloon.

But one thing he knew for sure: Jonas Covington, the biggest, richest, toughest cattleman in the county, was not going to crawl to Rance Gomer on his hands and knees and plead with him to get Belt before Belt got his son Jubal. Jonas needed Gomer's gun, but not badly enough to swallow all the pride and prestige accumulated over the years just to get some half-assed drifter to do a job for him.

Jonas had little confidence in his own ability to handle a weapon any more, especially now, his hand slowed by rheumatic pain. So, he would lay it on the line to Gomer, explain the deal, and he could take it or leave it.

While Covington was stewing in his own juices, Thomas Belt was cooling his heels in Whitton's jail. It didn't amount to much. The cell's only accommodations were a flat bench bed with a pad and blanket, and a wooden toilet bucket. Thomas didn't want to be there. He put up a strong argument against it, but the sheriff convinced him it was for his own good, and Thomas's choices dwindled.

"Locking you up is the only way I can protect you from Covington's outfit," Demp said to Thomas at the table in the corner of the Bang Tail Saloon.

"That's mighty nice of you, sheriff," Thomas said, "but I don't need protecting. What I hear, you didn't do much to protect my father the night he was murdered."

Whitton was caught off guard. He hadn't anticipated such a challenge from the man whose life he was trying to save. He hung his head, searching for an adequate response to Belt's accusation. "I was facing a mob," was the sheriff's weak defense. "I'm sorry it happened, but there's no way to change it. I can't tell you why I didn't take some kind of action that night."

"Well, would you like me to explain it to you, sheriff?"

Whitton tossed Belt a sharp look.

"You didn't do anything to stop it," Thomas went on, "because you were afraid you'd wind up where my father did–dangling at the end of a rope over a cottonwood limb."

"Those people were determined to–there was

nothing I could–"

"You were in charge," Thomas said. "You get paid for keeping the peace, but you buckled and ran scared, and let an innocent man die for nothing."

"All right," Demp said. "You've got reason enough to be riled at me."

"Riled?" Belt said. "I wanted to kill you. You're as guilty as Gomer and the others."

"I admit I was wrong not to stop it," Demp said. "But skinning two cats don't save the dog.

"That's why I want to be sure they don't get to you, so they can't do to you what they did to your father."

Belt studied the face of the man who confessed wrongdoing.

"Now," Whitton said, "I'm still going to put you in my jail."

Thomas had spent enough time behind bars to know he didn't like it, and was not eager to do it again. "On what charge?" he asked

"Well, I could charge you with disturbing the peace."

"Whose peace am I disturbing?" Thomas wanted to know.

With half a grin, Whitton said, "Mine. But, mostly because I want to be sure you're some place where they can't get to you."

Thomas heard the sincerity in the voice of the repentant sheriff. At the same time, he detected a sign of fear in the shadow of the sheriff's eyes. What was he afraid of? Surely, it couldn't be fear of losing the thirty dollars Covington paid him for playing sheriff. On the other hand, Thomas pondered, maybe it was because he was truly concerned for the safety of the man he was going to lock in his jail.

Thomas drained his coffee cup, and got to his feet. "I don't need protecting, sheriff," he said, "but you're the one with the badge. Let's go."

Thomas matched Whitton's long strides on their walk to the sheriff's office. Demp ushered him to the cell. He slammed the door on it, but left it unlocked. He would turn the key in the cell door lock later if he had to, to keep Covington out.

* * * *

Enter the raging bull

Any time Jonas Covington showed up in town it didn't go unnoticed. Bump Cauley saw him slam through the batwings of the Deep Six like a tornado looking for a town to blow away. Jonas rarely showed up at a saloon. He could count on one hand the times he was inside the Deep Six.

His eyes never wavered, aimed dead ahead at wherever he headed for, his neck stiff as a gun barrel. His big, raw-boned body, stone-carved facial countenance, and domineering, hellbent-for-leather determination caused people to quake in their boots even before Jonas said a word. When he opened his mouth to speak in his raspy, you-better-pay-attention-or-I'll-kill-you tone of voice, he got listened to.

Recalling his visit with Cecil, who came looking for Rance Gomer a couple of days before, Bump

Cauley showed no pleasure at the arrival of Jonas Covington. Bump knew Cecil hadn't gained any ground with Gomer, so he wasn't surprised when his old man charged in.

Jonas pounded the bar with a heavy fist with such force that it made glasses and bottles dance. Heads at the gaming tables swiveled around to see who did it.

"Where the hell is Rance Gomer?" Jonas roared.

Bump stared at him, unblinking. "Who the hell wants to know?" Bump asked.

"I'm Jonas Covington, and I–"

"I know who you are."

"–understand this is where Gomer hangs out."

Bump didn't hurry with his answer, swearing to himself that he wouldn't allow this raging bull to pull his bully act on him. He took a rag and wiped whiskey drippings off the bar. He took time to push his sleeve garters all the way up, almost to his shoulders.

"Did you hear me?" Covington shouted.

"I heard you, Mr. Covington. You likely don't remember the last time I heard you. It was the day you aimed a twelve gauge shotgun at my belt buckle, threatening to blow me to hell if one of my cows wandered onto your land. Half of my herd died because you wouldn't let them eat grass or drink water that you claimed belonged to you. The rest of them weren't worth much."

Jonas fidgeted, turned red in the face, and shot a mean-eyed squint at the smaller man. He could have broken Cauley over his knee if the notion struck him. "Let me tell you something," Jonas said, shaking a finger under the bartender's nose. "Maybe you don't know who you're talking to."

"I know who I'm talking to, but that don't cut no ice with me," Bump said. "Let me tell you something, Mr. Covington. I don't like you for all the reasons you already know. And if I don't like somebody, I don't tell them a damn thing."

"Why you scrawny little–"

"Most people who come in here buy something. If you want a drink, it's my job to get it for you. But, if you're looking for Rance Gomer, you'll have to find out from somebody else."

"Why, you yellow-livered–"

Covington reached across the bar and grabbed Bump by the collar.

The back room door flew open.

"Covington!"

Jonas heard somebody call. He spun around and saw Rance Gomer staring at him from the back room doorway.

"You looking for me?" Gomer asked.

Jonas shoved Bump against the back bar. To Gomer, he said, "We need to talk."

"What about?"

Bump straightened the front of his shirt, and watched the fuming Jonas stride briskly past the handful of card players. He pinned them with a glare, daring them to do anything about it. He met Gomer where he waited by the back room door.

Bump couldn't hear what they said, but he saw Covington and Gomer in a huddle. Gomer was waving his arms defiantly. Covington shook his head. Bump thought neither of them looked pleased about what was going on. Covington wheeled around, and walked away in a huff, raking a hand across his beet-red face.

"What's in it for me?" Gomer called to his back.

Covington kept walking like he was on a mission.

"I need to know if this is free or a paid job," Gomer said.

"Half a month's wages," Jonas tossed over his shoulder.

"Ten dollars?" Gomer said, incredulous. "Pretty skimpy pay for a killing."

"Take it or leave it," Jonas said.

Gomer shrugged. "I got nothing better to do. How about Pry and Eckles?"

"That's up to you," Covington said on his way out.

CHAPTER 19

Showdown at Whiskey Flats

"He's coming," Whitton said.

The sheriff met Redford in the middle of Parker Street half way between the jail and the Bang Tail Saloon.

"What's going on?" Redford said.

"Covington. He's on his way in. I don't know who all he's got with him, but he'll be hotter than a bull on a heifer when he gets here."

"Where is Belt?" Redford said.

"In my jail, like I said. He doesn't like being there. Claims he needs no protecting, but he didn't put up much of a fuss about it."

"Can I talk to him?"

"Help yourself. He's not locked in."

Whitton led the way into the jail. Redford

187

stepped through the doorway. He found Belt lounging on the pad in his unlocked cell. "How are you doing?" Redford asked.

"I'm all right."

"Whitton thinks you're better off here, and he's probably right, until after Covington is dealt with. He says Jonas is on his way in, and there's no telling who will be with him." He paused with a look into the eyes of Thomas Belt. "Thomas, there's no way to tell what might happen out there," Redford said. "You may have to face them before it's over."

"That's fine with me. I've got nothing to hide." Thomas took a moment to think out what he wanted to say. "The thing is, you know I'm not much good with a gun."

"I know that, and you know that, but they don't know that. Sometimes grit can beat a gun," Redford said. "It may come down to you against Gomer. If it does, don't say a word. Look him in the eye, and don't look away, like you're daring him to draw. Men like Gomer talk a lot, that's all. You beat him before. He remembers that. If you have to, aim for the chest. That's the biggest target."

Redford turned away. To Whitton, he said, "How much time do we have?"

"Well, it's a good hour's ride from the Circle C. Could be less, depending on how hard they ride"

Here came Jonas. Covington gigged his sorrel stallion into a lope, leading his charges to town. He was dead set on drawing blood from the body of Thomas Belt. Anybody who joined Jonas's vengeful pursuit of a man who did him no wrong he alienated by denying them access to water and grass for their livestock. He spent no time lamenting his action against them, but would welcome their help now.

And it didn't come. It was his grass, dammit! And his water! He wasn't about to give it away to a passel of blue-bibbed dirt farmers who made no contribution to the development of the country. They moved in after the hard work was done, expecting help from the people who struggled to make it livable.

Hell, no!

He raked his horse's flank with a spur, urging him forward. Cecil rode beside him.

"Why are we doing this, pa?" Cecil said.

"We never had any trouble," Jonas said, "till that black man showed up in town."

"What did he do?"

Jonas struck him with a deprecating glare. "He shot you, boy."

"It wasn't his fault. I—"

"Don't matter whose fault it was. He done it. Caused me to get into that ruckus with your brother. Now Nathan's gone."

"Pa, I don't think—"

"And now he's coming after Jubal," Jonas said. He cast a look at his eldest son, silently riding abreast on his other side. "You hear that, Jubal? He's coming after you."

Jubal couldn't muster a smile. His look was one of sadness.

A mile out of town, Jonas pulled up.

"When we get there," he said to the men behind

him, "you keep me covered. I'll do the talking. Gomer, I want you out of sight. Keep your eyes peeled. You'll know when it's time to come in. What we want is the black man. Nobody shoots unless you have to, but if anybody gets in the way, you know what to do."

Gomer peeled off and headed for the back side of town. Jonas raked a spur along his horse's flank, headed for the jail.

Redford's ears perked up at the sound of pounding hoof beats. "They didn't waste any time," he said. "Now, sheriff, what do you think about–" Before he could outline what he had in mind, he heard an angry voice outside the jail door.

"Whitton!"

It was Covington, and the sheriff knew it. There was no mistaking the demanding voice of the man whose pay he accepted for twelve years. He quaked at the threatening sound of Jonas's voice. "That's him," Whitton said, his eyes fixed on Redford.

"Whitton!" Covington yelled again.

Redford grabbed a shotgun from a rack on the wall, tossed it to the sheriff, and nodded toward the door. To Belt, he said, "Thomas, you stay put."

Whitton moved to the door, eased it open, and saw eight men on horses lined up ten paces from the jail door.

"Well, if it ain't the nigger-lovin' sheriff of the county," Googoo Pry chortled.

"What about it, Whitton?" Covington said. "I hear you got the black man locked in your jail for safe keeping."

"He's in here," Whitton said.

"Well, I want him," Covington demanded. "I want him out here in about two minutes or we'll haul him out of there."

Redford stepped out the jail door and stood beside the sheriff. He shot a steady gaze at the cattleman.

Covington, said, "What are you doing here, Redford?"

Redford spat a stream of brown tobacco juice and watched it form a small crater in the dust. "I didn't come to watch." He dragged a palm across his chin, wiping it clean of tobacco juice. "What are you doing here, Covington?"

"I aim to take that black man out of jail."

"Uh-huh. And do what after that?"

"Pay him back for what he's done to my family."

"What did that amount to?"

"He shot Cecil, caused me to shoot Nathan, and now he's coming after Jubal."

"Uh-huh." Redford nodded with a wry smile. "Belt told you that, did he?"

"Hell, no, but–"

"How do you know what he has in mind?"

"What the hell, Redford! I've got no truck with you. Why don't you get out of the way and go on about your business?"

Redford glanced at the mounted men huddled around Covington. The pickings must have been pretty slim, if the only men he could round were Pry and Eckles, a couple of skinny-assed saddle bums who never did anything without asking Gomer if it was all right.

Redford looked for Gomer, but didn't see him.

He wondered why. Cecil and Jubal flanked their father right and left. Rounding out the passel Covington thought could take Thomas Belt out of Whitton's jail were two Covington wranglers, Jess and Cotton. Jess was red-faced and fat. Cotton was skinny with a patch over his left eye. Neither of them looked like he was itching for a fight.

Redford figured they'd rather be throwing back whiskey at the Bang Tail than dragging some black man they didn't know out of jail for something they didn't care about.

"Pretty scroungy looking outfit you've got there," Redford said to Covington.

Covington stirred in the saddle, patience fragile as a cobweb. "I didn't ride all the way in here to jaw with you, Redford," he growled. "Either bring that black man out here, or we'll tear this place down and drag him out."

"Hear that, sheriff?" Redford said.

"I heard," Whitton said.

"Mr. Covington wants to tear your jail house down," Redford said. He spat again, pinning Covington with a challenging gaze.

To Whitton, Dan said, "Why don't you go bring Mr. Belt out here, sheriff–like Mr. Covington said?"

Whitton shot Redford a shocked look. He wasn't sure it was the right thing to do, exposing his prisoner to the mob that wanted him dead.

Demp stepped inside the jail, and a moment later, Thomas Belt appeared in the doorway. Facing the mob wasn't Belt's idea of the best way to go, but he figured Redford knew what he was doing. He could tell they were hot as a poker to see him dangle at the end of a rope.

Suspecting the big man in front was Covington, Thomas nailed him with a steady gaze, figuring Jonas cooked up this ruckus only to justify killing his own son.

Covington regarded Thomas with a quizzical squint. He wasn't certain this was the man he thought he'd see.

"That's him all right," Pry said.

"Yeah," Eckles put in. "It ain't hard to pick a nigger out of a wagon load of cotton."

"You tried to kill my boy," Covington said to Thomas.

"You've got it wrong, Mr. Covington," Thomas said. "Your boy had it in mind to kill me."

"You came to town looking for trouble, black man," Covington threatened, "and trouble found you! Cecil!" With an uneasy look at Redford, Cecil slid out of the saddle and made a tentative move toward Thomas.

"Cecil," Redford said, "you lay a hand on Thomas Belt and I'll kill you."

Googoo Pry took the distraction to go for his gun, but never got off a shot. A split second later he lay flat on his back in the dust, blood spilling from his mouth. Redford jerked his head around to see who fired the shot. Thomas was holding a gun. Smoke swirled out the muzzle.

Somewhere along the way, Thomas found time to practice.

"Well, Mr. Covington," Redford said, "here's the man you came to see dead. How bad do you want him?"

"Pa?" Cecil pleaded.

Covington's eyes narrowed to slits, glaring at Thomas.

"Give it up, Jonas," Whitton said.

"You slimy fever tick!" was Jonas's threatening response. "After all I've done for you."

Whitton answered him with a solemn nod. "I thank you for that."

"Pa, what do you want me to do?" Cecil cried.

"Dammit, boy!" Covington roared. "Do what I tell you!" He whipped out his gun and threw a random shot that hit Cecil in the head. Cecil collapsed in a heap and didn't move.

The next shot came from the gun of Jubal Covington, plunging into his father's chest. Jonas tumbled off his horse, both hands clutching the bloody gash, peering at Jubal in disbelief. "You– you'd shoot–your own fath–? I–" He fell over dead.

Cecil was already dead, and Jubal was the only Covington left. With no sign of the simple grin people expected, Jubal holstered the gun he'd fired only at turtles in a pond.

The two wranglers, Jess and Cotton, looked confused, but made no move to join the fight. They fell in behind Eckles.

Reining his mount west, Eckles wheeled around and flung a shot at Thomas that missed. Thomas answered with a shot and knocked Eckles off his horse. Eckles, flat on his belly, fired again. Thomas's shot to the chest put him away.

Jess decided it was time somebody else died. It turned out to be him. He ripped out his pistol and slung a couple of shots toward the jail door. A blast from Whitton's shotgun knocked him backward off his horse.

Jess screamed and died before he hit the dirt. Cotton made the unwise choice of joining the fray. He grabbed at his gun but never cleared leather. Redford planted a slug in his mouth. A bloody mess. Cotton slumped in the saddle, rolled off his horse. With a dead man's sigh, he breathed his last.

In a sudden move, Jubal whirled and threw a random shot at the black man. Belt fired again, and Jubal grabbed a handful of bloody arm, whimpering like the seven-year-old whose brain told him to fire the shot. Jubal tossed his gun aside and buried a spur in his horse's flank, heading west at full gallop.

"Black man!" The voice came from the middle of Parker Street.

Three pairs of eyes turned to see Rance Gomer standing there, spread-legged, coupling vengeance with wounded pride.

Thomas cast Redford a questioning look.

"He's calling you out," Redford said.

"Come on," Gomer yelled, "unless you're too scared to face a man!"

"Take a couple of steps his way," Redford said to Thomas. "It'll give him something to think about."

Thomas stepped onto Parker Street, faced the man he roughed up in the Bang Tail Saloon, expecting him to draw. Gomer did. Two shots were fired, neither from the gun of Rance Gomer. Gomer drew, but his gun went flying. He grabbed his stomach, fell to the ground, and died face down in the dust of Parker Street. Thomas Belt and Dan

Redford holstered their guns.

To this day nobody knows which shot felled the bully of Whiskey Flats.

Thomas turned for a look at Redford and Whitton.

"You did a good thing," Whitton said to Thomas. He held out his hand. Thomas grasp it in a hearty shake.

"I just remembered something my grandpa told me a long time ago," the sheriff said.

Redford said, "What's that?"

"If you look a polecat in the eye without blinking, he won't piss on you."

Redford grinned, slapping the sheriff on the back. To Thomas, he said, "I guess you'll be heading back to Mississippi."

"I don't think so," Thomas said. "I kind of like what I've seen around here. How about you?"

"I'm half way to Texas," Redford said.

"Ride easy, man," Belt said with a two-finger salute.

Redford turned away, and heard Whitton say, "That badge is still yours if you want it."

Redford responded with a casual wave and kept moving.

* * * *

An old nemesis shows up

After the last dog died at the Bang Tail Saloon, Eden said to Jake, "It's been a long day. Why don't you go get some rest?"

"No longer for me than for you."

"I own the place. I have to be the last one to leave."

"Like that sea captain who was the last one off the sinking ship."

"Something like that," she said.

"Well, good night then," Jake said. He ripped off his soiled white apron and tossed it under the bar. "I'll be here tomorrow."

"Goodnight, Jake," she said. "Jake."

"Yes, Eden?"

"I want you to know it means a lot to me–knowing I can count on you to be here tomorrow."

Jake offered a quick appreciative smile. He headed for the door, and traded nods with Redford who was on his way in.

"We're closed," Eden said as Redford pulled up to the bar.

"I know."

"What are you doing out this time of night?" she asked.

Eden knew he was relieved that the clash with Covington was over, but she waited for him to tell her.

As if he read her mind, Redford said, "It never should have happened. Thomas was getting a raw deal, and Covington was looking for some way to salve his conscience for killing Nathan. I couldn't stand by and let him hang Thomas for something he had nothing to do with."

"Thomas got Gomer?"

"He got Gomer. He could have got Jubal, but he

didn't."

"How come?"

"Ask Thomas."

Eden got quiet. Redford wondered why.

"I'd think by this time," she said, "you people would've worked out a better way to settle your squabbles."

She set out a glass, uncorked a bottle, and poured some whiskey into it. Redford fixed his eyes on hers, ignoring the drink.

"How did you handle things when you were six years old?" she asked. Did you take a gun to first grade and shoot the hell out of the kid at the next desk because he looked at you funny? Looks to me like you didn't learn a lot at Little Big Horn. War is hell, and nobody wins."

"It wasn't supposed to be that way," he said. That soaked-up mob wasn't supposed to hang Harvey Belt, and Thomas wasn't supposed to come looking for him. Covington wouldn't have anybody to put the collar on for what he did to Nathan. Killing Cecil was an accident. I can't believe even Jonas would shoot another son on purpose. But that's the way it panned out."

"Then his other son took care of Jonas?" she asked.

"Yeah."

He took up the whiskey, studied the bottom of the glass, as though expecting to find answers that he hadn't found any place else. He set the glass down and slid it aside. "Who do you think is in charge of who lives and who dies?" he asked.

Eden said, "The man with the gun?"

Redford gave his head a thoughtful shake. "Maybe. At Little Big Horn I heard men praying, pleading, with the hope of getting out of there alive. They made promises, swore they would be better men, husbands, fathers. "All good men, but they died anyway."

"So, what's the point?" Eden said.

"I heard some man say the day we're born, we start to die, a little bit every day. We try to live as long as we can, and take different roads to life. "Maybe the same is true of death–we take different roads to dying."

"That's too deep for me," Eden said. "What happened to the man who said that?"

"He died."

"What does that tell you?"

"Maybe you're right," Redford said. "Maybe the man with the gun is in charge. But who's in charge of him?"

"You might ask George Haskell about that." She pushed the glass back toward him. "So, what happens to Thomas now?"

"I don't know. I don't think he knows for sure," Redford said. "He said he wouldn't be going back to Mississippi."

"And Whitton?"

"I don't know that either. Covington won't be around to hound dog him anymore. I hope he'll talk to the mayor about staying on as sheriff."

"That leaves you. What about Dan Redford?"

"I've got to get out of here and head for Texas."

"Guilty conscience?" she asked.

"You might say that." His drink stood

untouched. "Have you heard from Cassie since she left?"

"Not a word. Have you?"

"No. And I won't. But I thought you might."

"Nope."

He took up the glass and spent a moment inspecting the bottom of it. "You know, you women have strange ways of making a man feel like a fool."

"What! Say that again."

"The way you crawled my hump about how I've treated Ashley."

"You had that coming," she said. "What else is on your mind?"

"Well, I've been thinking about Cassie lately. I don't feel real good about how I handled that. I think I might should've done more for her."

"You said she didn't want you to do anything." She cleared her throat.

When Eden cleared her throat, Redford learned she wasn't through talking. There was something else she needed to get off her chest.

"You know Cassie was in love with you," she said,

Redford cast her a how-would-you-know-that look. "How would you know that?" he asked.

"We talked. It's a woman thing. You wouldn't understand."

"I gave her no reason for that," Redford said.

"You didn't have to. Women love with their hearts, not with their eyes."

"Well, she had a funny way of showing it."

"Sometimes we women do funny things,

especially if we don't want you to know how much we care."

"Is that why you raked me over the coals about Ashley?"

She gave him a sideways look. "If we're afraid you don't care about us as much as we care about you, the cut gets a little deeper, and the wall gets a little higher between ourselves and rejection."

Redford lifted his hat and scratched his head with the same hand. "I guess that's why I've never been able to understand women."

"You're not supposed to. God didn't put you down here to understand us. "If you knew everything about us, you might not want anything to do with us." She fell silent for a moment. "Have you tried?"

"Tried?"

"To understand us."

"Not real hard," he confessed.

Eden went back to doing whatever got her closer to locking up for the night, collecting dirty towels, putting away washed glasses, wiping messy table tops, straightening the rows of bottles on the shelf behind her. Taking more time than it took, wondering if she should tell Redford some other stuff that was on her mind. "You ever think about getting married?"

"Doing what?"

"Married. You know–"

"I've thought about it." Her question came as a sort of shock. Redford had given it some thought, and tried to work up the gumption to toss the notion at her. Lonesome never went away by itself, and he needed someone to help give it a shove. "You know," he said with a deep breath, "it's funny you should ask me that. A man hopes all his life for some nice lady to keep him warm in the winter, and make sense of summertime. "If he's lucky, it happens one day, like a wild mule kicked him in the head, bringing him to his senses."

Eden gave him a look that said she wondered where he was going with that.

He told her. "You're the only woman I ever wished I could take home to mama," he said.

Eden's eyes got big, her mouth flew open. The bottle she was wiping slipped from her hands. It shattered on the floor, splattering her feet with the sticky brown stuff. She didn't bother to clean up the mess. "Say that again," she said.

"You're the only woman I–" He never finished the sentence. "You want to get married?" he asked.

She let it sink in. "I wouldn't mind," she said. "But not to you."

"Why not?"

"It would be easy to love you, Redford, but sometimes I don't like you."

"What does that mean?""

"Any man who gets a girl pregnant–" she said, fixing him with a steady gaze, "and leaves her to raise his daughter alone, then after she dies, farms his daughter out to relatives while he traipses around over the country playing cowboy and soldier– He's in a dead heat to do it again. Besides that, I wouldn't want to wake up one morning and find out you didn't come home the night before because some idiot with an itchy trigger finger shot you dead."

She paused, waiting for a response that didn't come. She wasn't through. "And there's something else you need to know,"

He looked at her, unblinking, half expecting her to confess to committing murder.

"You don't know me as well as you think you do," she said.

He opened his mouth, but the only word that came out was, "Eden–"

"Let me finish," she said. "You remember I told you about the man who rescued me the night my mama's house burned down. His name was Jack Claxton. He was a gambler with a mustache as thin as a tooth pick, piercing black eyes, and a cutting voice as cold as a hangman's heart. That's what my grandma used to tell me the devil looked like.

"Jack took me home with him that night. "At first he treated me nice. I don't know what happened, but after a while he hardly let me out of his sight. He locked me in the house while he made the rounds of the casinos.

"One night he told me a friend of his was opening a new club in town, and was looking for dancers. Jack told him I could dance. He didn't know if I could or not, but his friend hired me without seeing me. The club was in the basement of an old church. The dancing was taking my clothes off in front of a bunch of drunks who tossed coins onto the stage so I'd take off more. The coins were what I got paid. Jack kept them because he said I owed him.

"I was fifteen years old, and dumb as a post

about anything. I did whatever Jack said. I thought it was all right because he saved my life. But when he started selling my body, I found out how far down was.

"I finally got smart enough to know I didn't like what was going on. I couldn't leave because Jack kept the money. I started looking for a way out, hoping something good would happen to me. Something good finally did. My chance to escape came one night when Jack's friend called him away, and he couldn't keep an eye on me for a while.

"I had no idea how long he'd be gone. I knew I had to move fast. I ran half naked out the stage door and bumped into a man who said his name was Matt Fletcher. "He calmed me down, bought me some clothes, and paid for my supper.

"Matt offered me a job as an entertainer at his saloon in Whiskey Flats, Kansas. "I didn't know Matt. I had no idea where Whiskey Flats was, but any place sounded better than where I was. Matt Fletcher gave me my life back."

Her misty eyes and tremulous lips told Redford telling that story was difficult, but she had to tell it. "Jack never came after you?" Redford asked. She shook her head and it was his turn for throat clearing. He asked without taking his eyes off hers, "Will you still be here when I get back from Texas?" he asked.

"When will that be?"

"I don't know. But there's one thing I know for sure."

"And that is?"

"I don't give a rat's ass what you did before,

Redford said."I've got a few splotches on my record, as you reminded me. The you I'm looking at is the one I want to make a home for. I hope you'll accept my daughter as a friend, and help make a life for all of us. And I promise you, I will be home every night."

He watched her brush something from the corner of her eye. "If I found some place to settle down," Redford went on, "and maybe started selling beans and bacon at the Mercantile, would that be good enough for you to think about spending the rest of your life with me?"

"It would give me something to think about," Eden said.

"How long do you reckon you'd have to think about it?"

"How long do you reckon it would take you to start selling beans and bacon at the Mercantile?"

He tilted her chin, and kissed her on the mouth.

She came up for breath. "You better do that again."

Had she waited half a second longer, she wouldn't have had to ask.

The thud of heavy boots on the wooden floor, a sound that turns into something bad, caused Redford to look up. What he saw was a middle aged man dressed in black from head to toe. His black mustache was thin as the tooth pick Eden remembered. Like my grandma used to tell me the devil looked like."

Eden cast Redford a timorous look. "Claxton," she murmured with an uneasy breath.

Claxton pulled up at the far end of the bar,

piercing black eyes focused on Eden Fletcher.

Eden cringed, covering her mouth with both hands.

Redford made no move, waiting to see what Claxton was up to.

Eden had no chance to grow up, to be the girl teenaged girls were supposed to be–bouncy, happy, worried her hair may not look right, too long or too short, too curly or not curly enough. She had no girlfriends, and 'sleeping at a friend's' was a fun time she never heard of.

Claxton didn't allow her to date with boys her age, and she abhorred the frothy-mouthed men who paid to watch her take her clothes off. She didn't wear pretty dresses or slippers. Because she would be less attractive at the casino, he was careful that there were no marks on her body, causing his money well to go dry. His hand was always out for the money she earned–"for letting you stay at my house," he said.

Since Fletcher rescued her, she neither saw nor heard from Jack Claxton, and hoped she never would again. Her hopes were shattered when she heard his cold, cutting voice. "Well, now, ain't that somethin'?" To Eden, he said, "Are you going to introduce me to your friend?"

She made no effort to do so.

Claxton turned to Redford. "My name's Claxton," he said. "Eden and I go way back. Don't we, Eden?"

"Dan Redford," Redford said.

"Ah, yes," Claxton said with a tinge of irony. "The hero of Little Big Horn."

Redford studied the face of the man Eden described. He didn't like the arrogance he saw there and heard in his voice. How Claxton knew about Little Big Horn was no surprise. Redford wondered what Claxton came for, and when he would get around to it.

"You know," Claxton said, his voice hardly more than a whisper, "it's amazing how hard it is for a hero to hide. "I've been searching Kansas a long time, and I've heard about you, but– I'm a gambler, Redford. I would have bet the biggest pot I ever won I'd never be this close to the hero of Little Big Horn."

"What do you want, Claxton?" Redford asked.

"Well, like I said, Eden and I are old friends. I saved her life once when she was a young girl. Maybe she's told you about that. I took her in, gave her a home, helped her along, then at the first chance, she ran out on me. I can't help wondering why. I thought if I found her, she'd tell me."

Claxton was in no hurry. He had more to say. He said it to Eden, "I heard you headed west. From Kansas City, west means Kansas. Kansas is a big state, and you covered your trail pretty well. It took a lot longer to get here than I thought it would. But, you know what, darlin'? Finding you was worth the time and trouble. I've fixed up the place for you, and I've come to take you home."

Redford asked Eden, "Do you want to go?"

She shook her head no.

"Awe now, darlin', once you see it–"

Redford stayed put. "You've got your answer. It would be a good idea if you decided to go back to wherever you came from."

Claxton took his time about responding to the challenge. "You may be right," he said. He pulled aside the front of his coat, exposing the gun clinging to his right hip. "But I've come a long way, and it took a long time to get here," Claxton said. "I aim to take that lady home with me, and that's what I'm going to do."

Redford stepped out from behind the bar, locking his gaze on the face of the arrogant intruder.

Eden had heard enough. Shocked as she was to see Jack Claxton stroll into her saloon, she fumed with loathing for the man who made her a slave. She was not going any place with him. "You bloody bastard!" she hissed. "How could you have the gall to think I'd go any place with you?"

"Well, now, darlin'–"

"Don't call me darling, you son of a bitch! I'm not your darling and I never was." She grabbed the shotgun from under the bar and aimed it at his nose. I want you out of my place. If I ever see you again, I'll scatter your guts all over Kansas." She pulled the hammer back.

With a mirthless smile, Claxton threw up his hands in a token effort to calm her down.

Eden reached the boiling point, and calm was one thing she was not going to be. "Get out of my place and stay gone," she said, lifting the gun to eye level, "and save somebody the trouble of burying your stinking bones."

Claxton knew she meant it. He backed away slowly, toying with the idea of making a play, but he wasn't sure he could beat Redford to the draw.

And there was no way he could outshoot the lady with the twelve gauge. With all the bravado he could muster, he said, "This ain't over."

Redford thought it was time to tighten the cinch. "It's over."

Claxton backed out the batwings and bumped into a man he never saw before. A shotgun in the hands of an upset female was still poised at body parts he wasn't ready to lose. Claxton didn't stop to get acquainted with the man he bumped into.

Redford turned for a look at Eden. She still had the twelve gauge pointed at the batwings Claxton split on his way out, in case he came back.

"Redford!" The call came from outside.

It wasn't Claxton. He was last seen leaping into the saddle of a pale horse, high-tailing it out of town without a backward glance. Redford jerked his head around toward the door, but saw no one. He gave his head a dubious what-now shake. "I'll see who it is," he said.

"Careful," Eden said, putting the shotgun away. "That's him. The man who said he was going to kill you."

Redford headed for the batwings, and peered into the darkness.

"Over here," came the voice from the shadows filling the space between Doke's Hardware and Huskey's barber shop.

Redford figured it was the same man who slung a shot in his direction a few nights before, the one who was going to kill him in due time. He guessed this must be the time.

"Step out into the light," Redford said, "where I

can see who I'm talking to."

Coldwater took a moment to think about that. He didn't want to expose himself to the man he came to kill. Nor was he in a hurry to challenge the father of the girl he wanted to marry, but the matter had to be settled one way or another. He had to face him sometime.

Coldwater took a cautious step to his left where the flickering light from Doke's window fell on his face.

Redford moved onto the boardwalk. "You want to tell me why we're doing this?"

"Dad."

Redford was startled by the sound of the whispered voice from the shadow. Ashley? It couldn't be. Ashley was in Texas. But who else would call him Dad? He wanted to take his eyes off Coldwater long enough to look for the face that went with the whisper, but he dared not. "Ashley?" he asked in as soft a voice as the one he heard. There was no time to find out his daughter arrived on the last train that wheezed into Whiskey Flats on its way to someplace else.

"I love him, Dad."

Redford raised his right hand in a king's-ex motion in Coldwater's direction. Coldwater relaxed. Ashley was waiting in the shadows.

"What are you doing here?" he asked.

"I had to come, Dad. We buried Uncle Sid a week ago," she said. "I got away as soon as I could."

"Sid is dead?"

"He was killed in a shoot-out at a saloon. I'll tell

you about it later."

She threw her arms around her father's neck and gave him a healthy hug. "Oh, Dad," she cried, "I was so afraid Emitt might do something foolish because of what I said to him."

"What you said?"

"That's something else we'll have to talk about. I'm glad I got here in time."

"Ashley–"

"Please, Dad, don't go through with this. He's a good man, a little quick tempered, but I don't want to lose either of you."

"Coming all this way– Is that Coldwater–the one you wrote about?"

"Yes, Emitt Coldwater."

"He wants to marry you?"

"Yes."

"And what about you? Do you want to marry him?"

"Yes, I do."

"Does he know that?"

"Not yet."

He took a long look at the young man facing him from twenty paces away, right hand hovering near his gun–a man he knew nothing about, except for what he read in Ashley's letters. Coldwater rode all the way from San Saba to kill him for some reason Redford didn't know about. Was he a good enough man for his daughter–good enough for her to plead for his life? Ashley thought so.

"All right," Redford said. "Why don't you go tell him that?"

"Thanks, Dad," she said.

She left him with a peck on the cheek. "I love you."

Redford watched the two young people grab each other in a warm embrace. To Coldwater, he said, "You still want to kill me?"

"I guess not," the young man said.

Eden peeked over the batwings. To Redford, she said, "Now that's something you can be proud of."

With half a smile, he said, "Wet dogs don't ride."

"What does that mean?" Eden said.

"That's what my dad used say when he kicked a wet dog off the wagon because he'd be nothing but trouble."

"Why did he do that?"

"We had an old dog that would come up out of the creek and shake the water off, like dogs do. Dad didn't like him messing things up."

"So, does that mean this man is not a wet dog?"

"He'll do."

"Redford," she said.

"Yeah?"

"If you don't live to be ninety I'll kill you."

ABOUT THE AUTHOR

An accomplished author with many books to his credit, David A. Estes draws on his wide experience, from the cotton fields of Oklahoma and Texas where he grew up, to the islands of the South Pacific where he served as a United States Marine, to the market place in America where he retired from a career in broadcasting.

David writes westerns and mysteries, along with many other genres of novels and short stories. He lives on his family farm in West Central Missouri with two black Labs and a suspicious cat.